JON MOC

GW00721902

To ll ...

...fy !

Migrating Geese

An Anthology of Short Stories

Jon Moc Keepe

2... 20c8 !

Published by Jon Edward 2015
Ivy Corner,
18a Park Drive,
Rustington,
West Sussex BN16 3DZ

A CIP Catalogue of this book is available
from the British Library

ISBN 978-0-9930492-3-1 Paperback

Also available as an eBook
ISBN 978-0-9930492-4-8 Mobi

Front cover image:
©istockphoto.com/ Cameron Strathdee

Cover designed and typeset in Fairfield 11½pt
by Chandler Book Design
www.chandlerbookdesign.co.uk

Printed in Great Britain by
4 Edge Limited

C O N T E N T S

To Jean

*eternally grateful for your advice and
patience without which this work would
never have been completed*

Foreword

When developing my website and registering a domain name, I tried using combinations of my own names :

First attempt:
I tried John Sykes, and after forty-eight hours the site had twelve-thousand hits! The other John Sykes – rock-star guitarist, was I'm sure, suitably impressed.

Second attempt:
I tried my forenames John Edward, and a week later the site had eighteen-thousand hits! The other John Edward – TV Medium in USA, was I'm sure, impressed even more than the rock-star....

and so it was that Jon Moorthorpe became my pen name, after my birthplace.

* * * *

Family History research undertaken by my sister Margaret formed the basis of my first work 'The Gregory Journal' which was published in November 2014 to coincide with the 100th anniversary of the outbreak of the First World War. Primarily aimed at family and close friends, the project served to test my writing in these very early days of my 'apprenticeship', as well as learning more about the process of self-publishing. Only the reader can express an opinion on the level of success in either or both. Reviews from readers received to date can be seen here on the back page.

This second book 'Migrating Geese' is a collection of short stories which makes for easy reading when commuting, on vacation, or at bed-time - a perfect gift for loved ones at Christmas. Whether you're a smiley person or feeling a little sad, there is something here for everyone.

I would like to thank so many for their comments and advice, including Pauline Nolet for her superb proofreading and advice, John and Frankie Chandler for their off-piste guidance and excellent cover designs, Allyson Scanlon, Anna Ray-Jones,* Holly

Hill, Julia Macfarlane and the members of Bognor Writers for their support and encouragement, Dominic (Honeypot), Jeremy Good ** and all CHINDI members for allowing me to feed off their many and varied talents, Sylvia Bigger, Tom Millman, Maggie Taylor, Hanorah Murphy, Jacquie King, Margaret Walker, Richard and Sue Jeal, Mauricette Waddup, Michael (Honeypot), and finally Jacob Leak now aged ten, my 'poet in residence'. I hope to be forgiven by any I may have missed.

Each sale of 'Migrating Geese' triggers a donation to CancerWise which is a Chichester based charity dedicated to providing a wide range of complementary therapies and emotional support services to cancer patients, families and carers in West Sussex and South-East Hampshire. See www.cancerwise.org.uk.

Jon Moorthorpe

West Sussex,
July 2015

*   Anna Ray-Jones lives in New York and is the
    Author of ' Journey of Ashes' and many others.
    Follow Anna on Amazon.

** Jeremy Good lives in West Sussex and is the
    Author of 'The Butchers Son' also available
    on Amazon.

Introduction

Poem by Jacob Leak (aged ten)

So winter's approaching with thick snow and icy gales,
Its time once more for the migration to Wales.

Stops in Iceland and Ireland then we're ready to fly,
Once again in the air our spirits are high.

Having re-filled our bellies our bodies are strong,
Which is just as well because our journey's so long.

We might fly in an arrow shape playing follow
the leader,

Taking turns to go first to give the others a breather.

Our route takes us thousands of miles over land
over seas,

Following mountain ranges, coastlines, rivers and estuaries.

The flock will number many thousands as we travel,
Making such a racket with all our babble.

Soaring across the skies as light as a feather,
Carrying on through many changes in the weather.

When we reach Ynys-hir I shall search for
my partner,

We've come a long way but I'll honk until I
find her.

© **Jacob Leak** 2015

1

Migrating Geese

According to the Royal Society for the Protection of Birds (RSPB) approximately 700,000 geese migrate to the UK every year, mostly in the first two weeks of October. The geese fly thousands of miles from their breeding grounds across the Arctic Circle to escape the harsh winters and to feed on our saltmarshes, estuaries and farmland. The different types to be seen arriving in UK during this period include the barnacle, white-fronts, greylag and the brent with dark bellies. The greater number are white-fronts from Greenland mainly headed for the Ynys-hir Nature Reserve near Machynlleth in mid-Wales.

1973 Green Farm Cottage
(Twitchers Retreat)

"Look, son. From the west."

Jack handed the binoculars to Jeremy who fumbled with the focus then panned the sky until his face lit up with a broad smile, "Wow, that's awesome Dad. Never seen anything quite like that before. Are they all white-fronts do you think?"

Proud of his now twelve-year-old offspring for sharing the same ornithological interest, Jack was particularly happy that Jeremy so obviously still enjoyed the time they spent together in Wales every year. No doubt it wouldn't be too long before Jeremy's interest turned to girls as opposed to birds of the feathered variety – in all their forms. He took the binoculars back to take another look,

"I would say so son, because it's the third consecutive swarm and in such large numbers. Yes they must be."

Jeremy had shared his Dad's life-long passion for bird-watching from the age of nine. Since then they had always spent two weeks together near Ynys-hir to witness the arrival of the white-fronts. His headmaster was a friend of Dad's and although the second week of the trip to Wales generally coincided with half-term there were no questions asked about his absence in the first week – recorded as external nature studies no doubt.

The annual pilgrimage was to continue for a further eight years until Jeremy left home to study physics and engineering at Birmingham, again following in his father's footsteps except that Jack was a Brunel graduate. After three years of study at Birmingham Jeremy went on to join the engineering development team working on naval submarines at the Barrow shipyard. It was there that he first met Angela, who was secretary to the Programmes Director, and they eventually married six years later in 1990. Sadly they parted after ten years of marriage and were subsequently divorced in 2003 after Angela left to live with her girl-friend who had been their domestic help at home for nearly ten years.

Breaking up the family home in Barrow meant that Jeremy had to sell up and eventually he bought a two up two down terraced cottage in Newby Bridge at the southern tip of Windermere. Despite the beautiful surroundings of the Lake District he had little opportunity to enjoy his new surroundings as work occupied so much of his time, with long hours during the week and often Saturday mornings as well. It seemed rather like the old saying 'all work and no play...', as there was little time for any kind of social life. Most evenings it was after eight o'clock by the time he returned to Newby, and having parked the car, he would walk across the road to the Eagle and Child for something to eat. The landlord Richard always made sure the chef would stay on after nine if necessary; after all, Jeremy's custom could be guaranteed at least four evenings during the week and often weekends too. So it was that this routine became well established with Jeremy arriving late, eating alone with invariably only the barmaid for company. On the whole life was busy, and yet pretty lonely outside of work.

Soon after moving to Newby, he was at work when Uncle Harry called the office with the devastating news that Jack had suffered a heart attack at work and had died in the ambulance on the way to the Royal Preston Hospital. Within an hour of the call, Jeremy was heading south down the M6 towards Leyland to be with Mum.

In a little over two hours, he arrived home to find the lounge full of family and friends including the parish priest Father Desmond. Jeremy knelt by Mum's side – she was sat in Dad's favourite armchair. No one spoke, heads down, deep in thought. All he could say was, "Mum. Oh Mum… Dad, I can't believe it. I came the moment I heard."

Ellen just smiled and nodded. Then after what seemed like an age, but probably no more than ten minutes, everyone stood, formed a queue, took Mums hand, kissed her on the cheek and mumbled something like,

"Ellen, if there's anything… just say… ",

Even Aunty Joy seemed to be at a loss for words, something Jeremy had never known before.

A week later at the funeral, Uncle Harry addressed the congregation and spoke warmly of, "… the happy marriage for over forty years of my sister Ellen and Jack, … and of course I'm sure you would all agree that the closeness of the relationship between Jack and Jeremy was more like that of brothers rather than father and son."

Return to Twitchers Retreat

Barely twelve months after his Dad's funeral, Jeremy was made redundant as a result of cuts in the defence budget. Faced with more time on his hands he decided to continue with the trip to Wales and to Green Farm Cottage, the place which would forever hold such happy memories of the time spent there with his Dad.

It was the last Saturday in September, and having left home at 8 a.m. on the journey south, it wasn't until nearly half past nine that he pulled into the Charnock Richard Services on the M6. The weather forecast for occasional showers had turned out to be more like a steady and unrelenting downpour, and the fast-motion wipers had rarely been on slow since leaving Windermere. Armed with a large Americano and Danish Jeremy sat at a table in Starbucks next to the window overlooking the motorway, a pretty depressing sight with the still-speeding vehicles masked by the spray they threw skywards. Still, he thought, always look on the bright side and in another three hours he would arrive at Green Farm Cottage to begin a whole two weeks of peace and quiet. His mood lightened at the thought. Time for the road again.

Having re-joined the steady flow of traffic his mind mulled over everything that had happened over the past decade. There had been a number of life changing events, losing his Dad; his divorce from Angela; and more recently being made redundant and moving into the cottage at Newby Bridge.

Now aged forty-eight, Jeremy was tall, six foot two, still with a mop of thick dark brown hair. Middle age had inevitably brought a few extra pounds round the waist but otherwise he was healthy and pretty fit. With little prospect of finding a new job and yet much too young to retire, he occupied his time writing and had recently had two short stories published in magazines. He was now working on his first novel, and the tranquillity of Wales was only matched by the surroundings of the Lake District; perfection, he thought, in both places for a budding author.

He arrived at the cottage mid-afternoon and as he was unpacking the car Mrs Griffiths came down the lane from Green Hill Farm another half mile up the hill. She was a sweet old lady, barely five feet tall and Jeremy guessed well on her way, age wise, towards a congratulatory message from the Queen.

"Hello! Nice to see you again Mr Phillips. How's your journey been? Not too tiring I hope?"

Every year no sooner had he arrived than within minutes she would appear, and always with the same greeting. Jeremy had long since given up wondering how she knew he'd arrived; the farmhouse was too far from the cottage for anyone to hear let alone see, and there was no set time agreed beforehand.

"Good to see you too Mrs Griffiths. The drive down today has been pretty easy, despite the awful weather. How's Mr Griffiths keeping?"

He had always assumed she had a husband but in all these years he'd never been up to the farm nor seen anything of Mr Griffiths. The postman would often stop by on the way back down the hill for a chat, and apparently although there was regular mail to be delivered to the farm addressed to both Mr and Mrs, there was no sign of anyone other than Mrs Griffiths and a cat living up there.

She smiled and nodded, acknowledging Jeremy's concern. "He's been quite poorly in recent months you know. Doesn't get out much anymore. But thank you for asking. You'll find some milk, eggs, bread and tea in the larder, it will at least keep you going while you're settling in. I suppose you'll be going down to the White Lion later for something to eat?"

"Thank you so much Mrs Griffiths. It's much appreciated. Yes, I guess I'll probably take a stroll down into Machynlleth this evening then try to get an early night. I suppose the geese have started to arrive already?"

Mrs Griffiths put her hand to her mouth and looked up to the sky. "Oooh, my God yes, Mr Phillips. Last weekend I first noticed them. And in much greater numbers this year I wouldn't be surprised. Helluva racket they make too. So if I were you I'd advise an early night with a stiff whisky and a hot drink. That's what we do."

"I'll certainly bear that in mind Mrs Griffiths."

Jeremy wondered whether Mrs Griffiths had a first name. Even though he'd stayed at the cottage for a good few years now it had always been 'Mr Phillips' and 'Mrs Griffiths', friendly but at the same time quite business like.

Having said their goodbyes Jeremy went back indoors and put the kettle on for tea. It had been some hours since last he had a hot drink. He then unpacked, showered and dressed in a wool zip-up jumper, thick cords and his heavy walking boots. It could get pretty messy this time of year on the track leading to the cottage from the main road, and late nights were quite chilly if not downright cold this time of year. After arriving, he always left the car parked outside the cottage unless something really urgent cropped up before he was due to go home at the end of his stay.

It was a lovely evening, still quite warm when he set off for Machynlleth a little after six o'clock. On the way down the hill the number of geese flying overhead seemed to be growing in number with every stride he took, and having covered about half a mile Jeremy's attention was drawn skywards where there was an enormous flock of geese approaching from the direction of Ynys-hir, swirling, dipping, twisting, forming the most incredible and intricate patterns, and when directly overhead almost blanking out what was left of the rapidly waning evening light.

He stopped for a full five minutes watching them pass over and mouthing out loud, "Nothing I've ever seen can match that." Sod's Law strikes again, he thought, having left his camera on the table back at the cottage. Mrs G's description of one helluva racket was spot on, but even more so. The noise was absolutely bloody deafening.

Machynlleth and the White Lion

The White Lion Hotel is in the centre of the High Street near to the Clock Tower, and by the time Jeremy arrived it was nearly half past seven. He closed the heavy oak door behind him which immediately shut off the noise from outside. What a relief, and also what a pleasure to see that Gwynneth was still working behind the bar. She looked up and smiled, as though half expecting him to walk through the door. In the first two years of staying up at the cottage after his Dad died, Jeremy had got to know her husband, Huw, quite well. Both were in their late thirties with two children, a boy aged twelve and a girl of eight. Maybe tonight he would not be eating his meal in an empty room with no one for company.

This evening Gwynneth wore her dark brown hair brushed back into a French plait, with a black pencil skirt and white silk blouse. Jeremy had always liked the fact that her make-up was, in his opinion very feminine, but discreet, much like Angela had always been before their marriage breakdown. Gwynneth had been the regular barmaid at the White Lion it seemed like forever. The warmth of her smile and the inviting way she had of looking at the men in the bar made them all go weak at the knees. Just what landlord Albert Hughes needed to boost the beer sales from early evening through to closing time.

"Well, well, how nice to see you again. Here for the usual two weeks, is it? All the way to Welsh Wales now just for a pint of Reverend James I wouldn't wonder."

"Yes please Gwynneth. Good to see you too. Huw coming in later?"

Concentrating on pulling his pint, Gwynneth's smile was replaced by a much more serious look. She sighed, "Perhaps not. Lots happened since you were here last year. I'll tell you more later. He does still come in every now and then."

As if to put off saying much more, she continued, "Anyway, what news do you have? It's amazing how quickly the time seems to pass. Another year gone. My God." Gwynneth put his pint on the left-and corner of the bar. How on earth did she remember that's exactly where he always sat on a stool every year?

"Will you be eating tonight then? Seen what's on offer, 'ave you?" Gwynneth handed him the menu, leaning forward, smiling once more, and with that knowing twinkle in her eyes. He could see exactly what he might have hoped was on the menu but diverted his eyes, as it somehow felt not the thing to do, ogling a married woman's boobs, especially when he knew Huw so well.

"Welsh-style Dover sole is the chef's special tonight. Fancy a bit of that then?"

Gwynneth's extra friendliness left him slightly confused, and just a little embarrassed. What if Huw was to walk in right now? He handed the menu back.

"Yes the Dover sole sounds good to me, but no, on second thoughts, I think I'll go for my favourite steak and ale pie if you have it. With chips and veg, of course."

Waiting for his meal to arrive Jeremy sipped his second pint, curious as to what she meant by lots having happened since last year. He caught Gwynneth's eye as she turned back to the bar from the till. "So, you were saying?" She frowned and turned her eyes towards the group of customers stood at the bar then moved closer as if to confide something she didn't want anyone else to hear.

"Well, it's like this. Huw and I aren't together anymore. For the past ten months it must be."

"I'm so sorry to hear that Gwynneth." It was quite a shock to hear that she was now separated from Huw; they'd always seemed so happy together. They both fell silent, deep in thought. Then Jeremy looked at her, smiled and touched her forearm reassuringly, "So how do you manage work, with the children?"

Having composed herself Gwynneth returned his smile. "Mam puts them to bed for me and stays until I get home. Another pint, is it?" He nodded and emptied his glass. Jeremy turned his attention to his meal, while she was kept pretty busy for the next hour with the usual crowd of late drinkers. This was turning into a thoroughly enjoyable evening, something he'd been missing for far too long. The food, the company, what a change from the quiet of the Eagle and Child.

Jeremy's plate was empty, his glass was empty, and Gwynneth had rung the bell for last orders; it was just gone eleven o'clock. She turned from the till, sighed and with a shrug of her shoulders held out her hand for Jeremy's glass. As she took it from him their fingers touched for a brief moment, she had such lovely delicate fingers. "Thanks Jeremy. Hope you enjoyed it. Time for home, I think."

Jeremy stood. "A lovely evening as always, thanks to you. Would you like me to walk home with you?"

Gwynneth went out back and returned pulling on her coat. "Thanks. That would be nice. I'm just behind the museum, past the station, so you'll be going my way."

They strolled up the street in the direction of the museum. Jeremy talked a bit about his writing and his place at Windermere; then Gwynneth spoke about the children's school and how they were coping since Huw had left – apparently quite well. She didn't mention the reasons that led to the split, but obviously still felt very hurt. About a quarter of an hour after leaving the White Lion, they stopped outside Gwynneth's house. She took her door keys from her handbag.

"Well. 'Ere we are. Mam's asleep in front of the television I bet. Thanks for seeing me home Jeremy. It's so good to see you again. Maybe I'll see you tomorrow?"

"For sure. How about a coffee at the Chimes Café, about ten? Then I'll definitely be back in the evening, perhaps even have the Welsh Dover sole!" Jeremy took her hand and leaned forward to give her a goodnight peck on the cheek, but she turned her head to him and her lips met his full on, a soft lingering kiss, warm and so sweet, their fingers entwined.

Then they parted, each took a step back, fingertips touching, not a further word, eye to eye, just a warm smile exchanged. Then she was gone.

Jeremy stood motionless for what seemed like an age, still smiling, savouring the taste of Gwynneth's kiss. They had been so absorbed in their brief moment of passion he hadn't notice that it had turned quite cold, and had started with at first a few drops of rain that then turned into a steady downpour, the kind which quickly soaks one through to the skin, and yet he felt a warm glow that somehow protected him from the cold and increasing damp.

The only lighting into the row of cottages was from the junction with Maes Glas to the back of the museum; otherwise it was pitch black. He switched on his heavy-duty torch and headed back towards the main road and the two miles walk back uphill towards Green Farm. His head was spinning, recalling every last detail of the evening, thoughts dominated by imagining how things would develop with Gwynneth. Jeremy was thankful that true to his boyhood Scouting motto he was 'always prepared' in that his clothing was keeping him reasonably dry on this bleak, but at the same time magical night.

Thank goodness then that after about a quarter of a mile the rain stopped although it was cold and damp. It was slow going even though there was a good tarmacked path most of the way, the only light being from his torch. It wasn't until much nearer the turning into Drovers Lane that the pathway ran out and he had to walk along the grass verge. He regretted leaving the car at the cottage, but then another ten minutes and he would be indoors.

It had taken nearly an hour by the time he eventually opened the cottage door. He lit the oil lamp on the table then piled fresh logs on what remained of the fire. While the kettle was boiling on the stove he poured himself a tumbler full of a much-needed single malt, changed into his dressing gown and sat in the rocking chair next to the fire, glass in hand and a mug of steaming hot tea on the side table. Now he could relax. Dry once more, comforted by the warmth from the fire, the tea and whisky slowly adding to his drowsy feeling... his eyes became heavy. The only thing on his mind was the morning and seeing Gwynneth again.

Jeremy had fallen into a deep sleep in the rocking chair until he woke feeling the chill after the fire had died down. He rolled into bed and didn't move until seven o'clock. By eight thirty he was enjoying his second mug of tea and working out his schedule for the day. He had decided to drive into Machynlleth, have coffee with Gwynneth at the Chimes, then onto Ynys-hir, where he would spend the rest of the day until four-ish in the hide.

The Chimes

At a quarter to ten he was sat near the window in Chimes, looking out for Gwynneth, wondering whether she would turn up. He needn't have worried as spot on ten o'clock she appeared from behind the Clock Tower heading straight towards the café. Just as she came through the door his mobile rang. Jeremy recognised the number; it was Alice at Henshalls Employment,

"Hello? …, Hi, Alice. Thanks for calling. I guess it must be urgent for you to call on a Sunday morning. Would you mind if I call you back in say, five minutes? Okay, will do." He stood and pulled a chair out for Gwynneth,

"Hi. You look very nice I must say." He was aware that a couple of locals at the next table were hanging on their every word.

"Why thank you kind sir. That's good of you to say. How are you today? I did enjoy last night. Hope you didn't get soaked going home?"

Jeremy felt quite nervous. He hadn't felt like this in a very long time. There was so much to say, so many questions. But then he had to return the call from Alice, "Can I get you a coffee? Hope you don't mind, but I have just had an urgent call about some work?"

Gwynneth could see how uncomfortable he was. "The answer is yes and yes, please. Just a black filter coffee, and by all means return your call. I hope it's good news."

Jeremy ordered the coffee then returned to the table, "Thanks. I won't be long." He went onto the street outside and called Alice. By the time he came back, he'd been about ten minutes and Gwynneth's cup was empty.

"I'm sorry to have been so long. It's unforgiveable of me. Can I get you something else?" He sat and leaned forward looking, most anxious, not wishing to upset things before they had hardly got off first base.

"I'm fine for the moment, thanks Jeremy. It's important for you to pursue every opportunity that comes your way. I do understand. Well?" She smiled and put her hand over his, "Are you going to tell me?"

He relaxed, reassured by her response, "That was Alice. She's a headhunter in Carlisle. Wants to meet me in two weeks' time, on the Monday after I go home. I don't want to leave any earlier than planned so I put her off until the Tuesday. Apparently there's an opportunity with General Dynamics, a US company. She can't say exactly what the job is or where it's based. I suppose we'll have to wait and see"

"Well Jeremy it sounds really promising. I only hope it's what you're looking for. Although I'm pleased we can spend some more time together. There's so much I want to know."

"I know, and I feel the same. Hopefully we

can make the most of the rest of the time I'm here. Perhaps see you at least when you're working at the White Lion?"

"Yes, I'd love that Jeremy. I'm working tonight. Will you be down?"

"Yes. I'm going to spend the afternoon up at Ynys-hir. Should be down with you about six-thirty."

For the following fourteen days they saw each other at least once every day, and into the second week which was half-term, the children went to stay a few days with their grandma. A month ago neither Jeremy nor Gwynneth could have seen this coming, but they were falling in love.

Their good night kisses had grown more passionate as the days passed, and eventually on the Thursday evening Jeremy stayed over with Gwynneth. The following morning they lay in bed chatting about how good they both felt, that they had each never imagined they would find such happiness again.

Gwynneth turned towards him, "Jeremy?"

He turned towards her, "Yes my darling?"

"I didn't want to say anything before, but you should know that the reason for Huw and I separating was that he was having an affair with the daughter of his boss at work. She's fifteen years younger than me."

"Oh sweetheart, I'm so sorry. I guessed it must be something like that. Still we've now found each other and there's so much to look forward to."

Gwynneth sighed, then smiling, turned his way and they fell in each other's arms, "I hope so. I really do hope so."

Newby Bridge and Beyond

Following his return Jeremy met with Alice in Carlisle and he learned that the job vacancy was with a UK subsidiary of General Dynamics based in South Wales, and the work sounded very interesting. The first of the good news was the new love in his life, and then to top it all he would be able to move to Wales which would enable him to see Gwynneth almost every day, and who knows where that might lead? Jeremy couldn't remember ever being so happy.

The following three weeks were largely taken up with further meetings with Alice, with GD human resources, then the engineering and programmes directors. The package on offer included a very generous re-location allowance, and everything was working out just perfectly. Jeremy accepted the offer to start work the second week in November.

He called Gwynneth every day to give her the latest news, and they talked at length about how things might develop in the coming months. However he became a little concerned when into the first week of November both Gwynneth's landline and mobile weren't answered, and this continued for the rest of the week without them speaking. Time had run out for Jeremy and he had to continue with the move into temporary accommodation in Usk arranged by the company. The lack of contact with Gwynneth over the past week was worrying and he had great difficulty in concentrating on preparing to start the new job. So on the Sunday morning he called the White Lion. The landlord answered,

"Albert Hughes. White Lion. How can I help you?"

At last Jeremy had managed to speak to someone. "Good afternoon Albert, Jeremy Phillips here. How are you?"

"Ah yes Jeremy. I'm fine thanks."

"Albert, I've been trying to contact Gwynneth for the past week, but her numbers don't seem to be working. Can you help? I've now moved to Usk for my work."

The line went quiet. After what must have been two minutes Jeremy assumed they had been cut off and was replacing the receiver when Arthur answered,

"Hello? Jeremy?"

"I thought we'd been cut off. Yes I'm here."

Albert continued "Well Jeremy I can't be of much help I'm afraid. I think it would be best if you come up. Next weekend? Sorry about that Jeremy but I've got to go."

Jeremy decided to try Gwynneth's numbers again at the first opportunity into the week, and then follow up with a trip to Machynlleth at the weekend. That evening it was back to the Eagle and Child routine dining in an otherwise empty restaurant at the Nags Head. With the frustration of being unable to contact Gwynneth, starting the new job, and now feeling very alone again he felt absolutely drained, quite depressed.

The first day at work wasn't all that demanding, and once back in his room he tried Gwynneth's home number as well as her mobile, but again there was no reply. This was getting unbearable; something must have gone terribly wrong. The sooner Friday afternoon came and he could find out for himself what had happened to Gwynneth, the better. He just couldn't get her out of his mind. On the Friday morning he had already packed a small bag ready for the weekend, and by three o'clock everyone had pretty well finished work and he was once again on the road up the A4042.

It was half past four by the time he arrived at the Clock Tower. He parked the car and walked in the direction of the museum. He thought it better to go on foot so as not to attract attention in the street outside Gwynneth's home. Jeremy really didn't know what to expect. If she answered the door, what would he say? The last time he was here they had slept together and it seemed as though they were very much in love with each other, so what had changed? He felt sick with anxiety at the prospect of learning the truth of what had happened and his difficulty in getting to speak to Gwynneth for the past two weeks.

He was just about to knock when the door was half opened and there was Gwynneth. Gone was the beaming smile, gone was that knowing twinkle in her eyes. She looked so tired, worn out.

"Jeremy…, I'm sorry not to have spoken to you. I just didn't know what to say…, It's Huw. There was a terrible accident at the gas works and he was very badly injured. He's lost his sight and will be in a wheelchair for the rest of his life. I'm so very sorry. I had thought we would… " She burst into tears and closed the door.

Much as he had on that first night, he stood motionless, staring at the door, but this time was different. He was stunned, his mind trying to come to terms with this devastating turn of events. After what seemed like an age, Jeremy turned and headed back towards the car, heading for an uncertain future.

2

Deep Joy

Pre-School

Joseph had been Barry's best friend since they had started at Buckles and Bows Nursery on the same day, when they weren't quite five years old. It had been the best news ever when a year later they learned that they would be going up to 'Big School' together.

St Barnabas First School

The two pals were now in class 3M, and after Mrs Coleman retired Barry's Aunty Joy was appointed Headmistress at St Barnabas. All their classmates were in awe of the new Head who was ever so tall and quite stern looking. She was only ever seen to smile when speaking to other teachers, parents or the school caretaker.

Soon after Aunty's appointment it became obvious to Barry that all his classmates were being very careful of what they said in front of him in case he repeated any comments about his Mums sister when he was at home.

The two friends were inseparable, and were more often than not to be found together in the playground, chatting about the great many things that were important for seven-year- old boys to understand. Most of the time they didn't mix with the rough boys.

Soon after the Easter Holiday Joseph asked Barry "Is it really true that the Head is your Aunty?"

"Yes. She is my Aunty, my Mum's sister."

Joseph was reassured by this answer, and indeed, was proud that his bestest friend's Aunty was the headmistress at his school. His Mum would be very impressed.

"Well, Barry, why I asked is that My Mum's friend is Mrs Butterfield, they live two doors away from us, and Mum says to call her Aunty Pauline but she's not really my Aunty. Why's that do you think?"

"Dunno" Barry replied, then continued. "What I can't understand Joseph, is that Aunty calls other boys by their names like, I heard her shout,

'Terence Spratley, no running in the corridor' or 'Derek Fairchild, for goodness sake, stand up straight. Head up, shoulders back. What would your Mother say?'

But seems she's forgotten my name, and whenever she sees me, just smiles. It's like being invisible, or maybe do you think she can't remember? Aunty is very old."

At home that afternoon he decided to ask Mum why Aunty Joy knew everyone in the whole school but couldn't remember his name. Mum was in the middle of baking, but nevertheless was thinking carefully about Barry's question. She always chose her words carefully, as she could never be quite sure where Barry's questions might be leading.

He always began 'Mum? Why...?'

And today it was "Mum? Why doesn't Aunty know my name?"

Mum put the tray into the oven, this one was going to be easy, or so she thought.

"She does know your name of course sweetheart. But it's probably because Aunty doesn't want to appear to favour you because you're her nephew. As she's the headmistress at your school she mustn't show it in front of the other boys."

"Mum? What's a nephew?"

"Well, that's because you're my son and Aunty is my sister. So you're what is called a nephew."

"But I don't understand Mum. It's all very difficult, and I'm only seven and three-quarters and not eight until my Birthday!"

Mum smiled and shook her head. Quiet

descended on the kitchen for over five minutes while Barry tried to figure out these very complicated relationships. It was just all too much, so he decided to try another question.

"Mum? Why doesn't Aunty have any children?"

"She's just been too busy darling, and in any case she's not married."

Mum thought this would put the relationship questions to bed, but she was wrong.

"Mum? Do you have to be married to have children?"

Mum wondered where on earth this was leading. (Barry's Grandad Walker always thought his curiosity a healthy sign 'Mature beyond his years that lad,' he always said.)

"Yes. You do have to be married to have children darling, just like Daddy and me."

"But why Mum?" Barry was most insistent on getting to the bottom of this. It was very important to properly understand grown-up things when you're only seven and three-quarters.

Mum sighed and looked over at Dad who was reading his paper, and as usual saying nothing. Barry was sure his dad was smiling at something in the paper. Then Dad had a fit of coughing.

"Well sweetheart, it's like this, to have children there has to be a daddy to go out to work and earn money to buy food to feed the children."

Now I think I understand, thought Barry, although something still didn't quite add up.

"Mum? If Aunty Joy had a Dad to go out to work, what would I call him?"

"He would be your Uncle sweetheart."

Mum, Dad, Aunty, Uncle. Yes now it all makes sense. Barry looked triumphant.

"Mum?" Mum was getting a bit fed up with all the questions, "What is it now?" she demanded,

Barry looked puzzled,

"Well, Mum, today at school Joseph heard Mrs Davies say Aunty Joy is expecting a baby. So what's my Uncle's name?"

This was all just too much. Mum looked imploringly at Dad,

"Can you hear all this? I think he's forgotten he has a dad."

Dad held his paper even higher so that it covered his face.

Mum was clearly not best pleased. "And what, James Walker, may I ask, do you think is so funny?"

Dad burst out laughing, almost choking, "And my guess is that Aunty Joy would like to know Uncle's name as well!"

3

Smiling People

It was now October and Grandma had been at the Happy Days Care Home for almost six months. She had initially been very unhappy at the prospect of leaving her home but at the time had accepted the move on the basis that it was to be temporary respite care. However, by now she couldn't remember how long she'd been there and most of the time seemed quite happy and content.

David visited his grandma two or three times a week, so it wasn't long before he got to know the other residents who were on the whole a nice bunch of people, and always seemed pleased to see him. He particularly liked Ursula, who invariably greeted him with the same 'Hello Daddy. Mummy not come with you?' and Stephanie, who both made him laugh.

Arthur Hardcastle was the resident wag, meaning that he had a very dry sense of humour that had nothing at all to do with the partners of millionaire soccer players. He was what one might say a well-rounded older gentleman in that he was not only rather round physically but also widely travelled. His handle bar moustache was acquired during his twenty years in the Royal Artillery, finishing his career as Battery Sergeant Major.

Often described by Arthur as 'away with the fairies', Stephanie Gorringe had in her time been a leading lady in many productions at the Grand Theatre in Leeds, as well as touring with the Royal Shakespeare Company. She was tall for a woman, about five foot ten, and always wore a white silk nightdress decorated with pink bows, which she insisted was her ball gown. She rarely engaged in conversation with anyone other than the Manager, Mrs Bates. Most of the time, in the day and early evening Stephanie 'floated' from the lounge to the garden then into the entrance hall, arm outstretched, her eyes fixed skywards outdoors or on something high on the ceiling inside. All the time making a strange cooing sound.

Jennie in Room 11 opposite Grandma was the one person at Happy Days who Grandma positively disliked, intensely. Jennie always protested that her proper name was Jennifer, which of course only encouraged everyone including Mrs Bates, to continue calling her Jennie. She was barely five foot in height, almost the same measurement round the waist and wore old-fashioned NHS wire framed glasses. She had never married and probably never had a boyfriend, even though she often boasted about the never ending queue of lovers seeking her favours. Most of the time she looked thoroughly miserable but always smiled broadly whenever she saw Grandma.

Every time that Jennie made an appearance in the sun lounge Arthur would call out so that everyone could hear, "Watch out. Here comes Jennie the Giant Peach."

David, his Mum Janet, and the rest of the family were now well used to hearing that Grandma was being left alone for long periods with nothing to do, and that she never had visitors like the other residents. She was always pleased to see David although she wasn't at all sure who he was or what his name was. He always greeted her with the same,

"Hiya Grandma. What you been doing?"

Grandma positively beamed at this stranger sitting next to her, although he did look vaguely familiar.

"Ello love. Not been doing much today. Linda helped me to shower, then one of the others, never seen her before, came and did my hair."

"But Grandma, it's only twelve o'clock. You seem to have been pretty busy so far today, and your hair looks very nice. Mum will be pleased when she comes in later."

"Is it only twelve love? I thought it was at least three and I haven't had any lunch. It's about time your Mum, errrmm, whatsername, came to see me. She hasn't been here for weeks. Don't like it in here. Bloody miserable lot, always smiling at me. Don't know what they've got to be so bloody happy about."

Grandma pointed at Jennie, "See that one over there, Jennie's her name, although Mr Hardcastle calls her 'the clockwork orange' or something like that. Well, she never stops bloody smiling at me all day and all night, I'm sure, and when she passes me in her wheelchair she winks at me. I think that's because she takes money out of my purse and steals my other things. Soon there'll only be the bed left in my room. Thinks I don't know what her little game is. Is it today you're taking me home Keith?"

David had become quite used to Grandma swearing, although it was completely out of character. For the past twenty years he'd never even heard as much as a 'damn' pass her lips. She'd always been the life and soul of the party. Until recently she had been a Sunday school teacher at St Mary's Parish Church and sang in the choir. Grandma had devoted her whole life to bringing up her own children Janet and Keith, and then in later years she always took a very active interest in the grandchildren. Grandma had always put others before herself. Her deteriorating health was heart breaking for everyone who had ever had the pleasure of knowing her in the past.

Occasionally Janet saw Grandma's GP Dr Prentice, who was always so understanding, "How do you think your Mum is? She seems to have settled in very well. You know the dementia will get worse over time, but as long as there are no other major health issues, she will probably continue to be pretty happy here for many years."

Janet was close to tears. The years of worrying about her Mum was also affecting own her health and her GP had prescribed anti-depressants, which helped,

"Yes, she does seem to be quite happy most of the time, but then she gets very frustrated when she can't remember. She was upset this morning when she had a words with Jennie in the room opposite. Mum is convinced that she goes into her room and steals money, and other things seem to be going missing. They clashed this morning when Mum accused Jennie of taking her china ornaments."

Dr Prentice nodded and smiled reassuringly. "Yes. I know. You will probably find the ornaments in a cupboard or the back of a drawer, and as for the money, she probably buys newspapers, magazines or sweets from the trolley. It's very sad but all too common these days. My own father is very much the same. Does she see much of Keith these days? She always speaks so highly of him."

"I know," replied Janet. "Mum sees Keith about every three to four months, at most half a dozen times a year. He's always so busy."

Later that week when Janet visited her Mum she decided to look through the wardrobe and all the dressing table drawers but found no trace of the missing ornaments. She went downstairs to the Managers office and spoke to Mrs Bates about her concerns. Mrs Bates was always ready to listen to relatives and to reassure them,

"I do understand Janet, and I'm sure you'll find that the ornaments have probably been broken. I'll check with the staff to see if they know anything. As for the money she definitely has a newspaper every day, takes The Peoples Friend, and I have seen her buying a bar of chocolate from the trolley. It's quite common with dementia sufferers to mislay personal items and cash. I'm sure it's nothing to worry about."

"Thanks for that Mrs Bates. However I'll have another look in Mum's room to see where she keeps her money. I buy all her toiletries and anything else she needs, so I can't see how she spends twenty pounds a week on newspapers, magazines and some sweets. By the way, how's your son Norman? I haven't seen him lately."

"He's fine, thanks Janet, but this time he'll be away for quite some time. In fact I'm not at all sure he'll be back much before I retire."

In the first week in December David called in to see Grandma on his way home from work. Grandma seemed quite excited about something and whispered "Can you take me upstairs love?" She looked round at the others sat in the sun lounge then nodded her head in the direction of the hall, and the lift up to her room on the first floor.

Once in the lift she continued with her confidential whisper holding her hand to her mouth, "I heard them talking at breakfast time. Apparently Ursula died during the night. Now Jennie's going to another hospital this morning and won't be coming back. Thank God for that."

The lift stopped and Grandma put her finger to her lips so as not to say anything further. As they stepped out onto the landing David was confronted by a policeman outside Room 11. Grandma opened her room door and went in, but David hesitated, curious as to what was happening. Then the PC opposite stood aside to allow two male nurses to push Jennie out in her wheelchair towards the lift. She was held in the wheelchair with what looked like some kind of restraining belt around her middle.

As they passed David, Jennie turned her head and smiled, and of all things winked at him! The Giant Peach's chubby hands clasped her handbag, her Teddy, and a china ornament, just like the one Grandma used to have.

4

Edward and the Meaning of Life?

Born in Worthing in the early months of the Second World War, Edward was the first of three children and he was to be followed by two sisters, Margaret and Kathleen. The family later moved to Chichester to be nearer to Dad's work. The children enjoyed a very happy childhood with two loving parents who undoubtedly sacrificed a great deal throughout the period until rationing ended in 1954.

Now, at the age of fourteen, Edward faced the prospect of leaving school at Christmas, just before his fifteenth birthday. One evening after dinner the two girls made themselves scarce as Mum and Dad obviously had something important to say. It was left to Dad to take the lead.

"You're leaving school in two weeks' time son, and

to my mind that's much too young these days. Anyway, I've been talking to Mr Mosby in the Observer office, and he wants to talk to you about a job."

In fact Edward was quite relieved as most of his classmates were going to work at the Rudge bicycle factory, while he'd always fancied trying something different. Although he wasn't at all sure what that might be.

"You'll see, it's all for the best son. At least go and see Mr Mosby. The Observer office is on the opposite side of the road from the Market. There's the print works at the front and the Editor's office is at the back. He's expecting you at ten o'clock tomorrow morning."

Edward was nervous at the prospect of meeting the famous journalist who was quite the best known celebrity in the area. It was also his first involvement with the adult life of work. A couple of minutes before ten he knocked on the door to the office, no answer. Before knocking again he put his ear closer and could hear someone speaking so he waited until it went quiet then tapped on the door a second time – the door opened wide.

"Come on in lad."

Mr Mosby reminded him of Grandad Simpson. Not very tall, not much hair and with glasses balanced precariously on the end of his nose. He was smoking a pipe. Grandad's pipe always made Edward cough, but on this occasion he resisted the urge as it was no doubt not very polite. The work sounded very exciting and the very informal chat ended with a smile and an outstretched hand. This was new, he'd never had a grown-up handshake before.

"I'd really like you..." pause to cough...,

"to start..." long drawn out puff puff, then suck, then another fit of coughing.....,

"as soon as possible. What about first thing after Christmas lad? Come back here at nine o'clock on the second Monday in January."

"Yes Mr Mosby. Thank you Mr Mosby." Edward's smile told it all. Dad would be pleased.

After Christmas Edward arrived at the Observer office at a quarter to nine, nice and early on his first day. He was still wearing his first pair of long trousers which by now were getting a bit on the short side; however, during the holiday Mum had knitted him a new pullover, and he was also now the proud owner of a new navy duffel coat. It had been a choice between new trousers or the coat, and given the weather at this time of year the duffel was what was needed most. On this, his first morning at work, it was cold outdoors with a thick frost.

Mr Mosby explained what he expected of Edward, which apparently consisted of cycling round the local villages collecting information from various addresses on the list which Mr Mosby would leave on the typewriter each night before he left.

He was introduced to the folk on the printing side of the business. Mr Barraclough, who Edward already knew, was a short, fat man, with a mop of dark brown hair. He was always very jolly, a very smiley kind of man. He had managed the print shop for over thirty years. His assistant, Janet, was a much younger lady, tall and with blonde hair. Edward had never seen blonde hair before, other than in the films at the Picture Palace on Saturday night.

Mr Mosby called Mr Barraclough Bert; Edward was to call Mr Barraclough Mr B; everyone called Mr Mosby Mr Mosby; Mr Mosby and Mr B would call Edward lad; but at least Edward was allowed to call Janet, Janet. There was no doubting where Edward stood in the pecking order.

The rest of the week was spent shadowing the Boss, watching and listening, taking careful notes of everything he heard, and saying nothing other than "Thank you Mr Mosby." This activity meant that Edward got to sit alongside Mr Mosby in his car, and as the only other means of transport previously had been the bus, this was yet another new experience. This was indeed all very exciting, and he could hardly wait to tell Mum and Dad.

The following Monday morning, Edward arrived at work only to find Mr Mosby already hard at work before setting out on his usual weekly round of visits to the Police Station, St Richard's Hospital, the Cemetery, then finally the Fire Station. He looked up from his desk as Edward settled into his chair.

"How you doing lad? And how's your Mum and Dad keeping? Well I hope."

Mr Mosby turned back to his papers not waiting for, nor expecting, an answer.

"Today I want you to call at the cemetery to see what new customers are on Mr Morgan's list from the weekend. After I took you there last Thursday he knows who you are, and he'll be expecting you."

Edward smiled, "Yes Mr Mosby." He had enjoyed the first visit to the Cemetery as the Superintendent, Mr Morgan, reminded him of Christopher Lee in the Dracula film, tall, thin, with longish black hair and funny teeth.

Mr Mosby continued with the usual barrage of questions, with hardly any chance for Edward to squeeze in a reply.

"Did you know Mr B before you came here lad?"

"Yes Mr Mosby. He's a Sunday school teacher at the Chapel, and Dad knows him from the Operatic Society and says Mr B is a fine baritone. Dad plays the piano in the orchestra."

Mr Mosby puffed on his unlit pipe and muttered

something like "I know, and very familiar with Gilbert Sullivan I've no doubt."

Edward was quite taken aback by this. How come both Mr Mosby and Mr B knew Gil O'Sullivan who'd been in his class at school? After all the O'Sullivans only moved here from Portsmouth less than a year ago.

Mr Mosby was in a hurry today so thankfully hadn't re-lit his pipe, just puffed away as usual. He picked up his briefcase and waved as he went through the door "Cemetery" he called over his shoulder.

"Yes Mr Mosby."

Other than on Edward's first day at work the interconnecting door separating the two sides of the business was always locked, presumably on the print room side. On Wednesday morning just before lunch he was in the office and finishing off a wedding report when his concentration was interrupted by Mr B roaring loudly at the top of his voice whilst at the same time Janet squealed and giggled uncontrollably. The roaring and the giggling were accompanied by the sound of chairs and furniture being moved. Then, after a couple of minutes Mr B started to sing one of his favourites from The Sound of Music......

"The hills are alive with..." The rest was drowned out by Janet's shriek, almost scream like, "Mr B, oh you're so wonderful. Encore. Encore."

"...for a thousand years..."

Strange that, thought Edward. He'd always associated The Sound of Music with Julie Andrews, so to hear it sung by a deep baritone just didn't seem right somehow. Also, who would have guessed that Janet was into musicals? Rock and blues was more her scene. This was the last thing on earth he would have expected to overhear at work, it sounded so funny he was tempted to laugh out loud, at the same time thinking what on earth would Mrs B make of all this?

5

Loneliness of the Long Distance Grandpa

David

Richard and Samantha Carter moved to Roslyn, New York, after they married ten years ago, and two years later their son David was born. They live in a detached white-fronted house with the front lawn bordered by a wooden picket fence and the mailbox next to the gate. David, now seven, their only child was born two years later.

One day at school, Jerry Simpson had taunted David most of the day, whenever he got the chance. He was well known for seeking out the more sensitive boys at school. The teachers were well aware of the bullying but seemed powerless to do anything about it.

Jerry was head and shoulders taller than most of the guys in class and he just loved playing the tough guy, always of course provided he was backed up by his cronies. After two semesters of being continually picked on, David's nerves were on edge whenever Jerry and his gang approached him

"How many have you got then Carter? We've all got two and they take us to the ball game or fishing at weekends, and sometimes we take in a movie. Where does yours take you? Nowhere, I bet. That's because you don't have a grandpa."

This was the very worst thing anyone could say to David when he wanted more than anything to see Grandpa Swanson, but he couldn't remember if he ever had. Tears welled up in David's eyes, but he was determined not to show it and at the same time thinking, 'Why me? Why can't I have a grandpa just like the others?'

The moment the bell rang for class to be over David ran towards home down Independence Avenue, crying all the way. Nearer to home he almost bumped into Mrs Sullivan who was on her way home from shopping at the convenience store on the street corner.

"Hey! Slow down young Davey Carter. And be careful, look where you're going, this is a very busy road here." Mrs Sullivan, the next-door neighbour, always called him young Davey.

"Come now, tell me. Why are you crying? What's wrong?"

David looked up at her, she was very tall. Mrs

Sullivan must be very old, he thought, because she had white hair and her son was about the same age as his own dad.

"The guys at school say I don't have a grandpa. But I'm sure I do. Mom says Grandpa Swanson lives in New York City, but I've never seen him Mrs. Sullivan, and Grandpa Carter has gone to live with Jesus. Do you think Jesus lives near my other grandpa?"

"I guess he might well do young Davey." Mrs Sullivan was always very kind.

When Mom answered the door she found David sobbing, quite inconsolable. She hugged him and patted him gently on the back of his head,

"There, there honey. What is all this about?"

"Mom. Oh Mom, the guys in my class never stop talking about their grandpas' and saying I haven't got one.

"You mustn't listen to them honey. Just ignore them. Don't forget you do have two the same as every other boy in your class. It's just that Grandpa Carter now lives with Jesus and Grandpa Swanson lives in New York, and that's a long long way away."

David had settled a bit now, "When can I see Grandpa Mom?"

"Well that's the problem you see. Because he lives so far away, New York is like a different country.

With your dad and I so busy with work, unless Grandpa comes here.......As I say, it's just too difficult for us to see him as much as we'd like."

"But I never see him Mom."

Grandpa Swanson

Samantha's father, John Swanson now aged sixty-five, had lived in his apartment on Hawthorne Street in Brooklyn for the past fifteen years since his wife Kate died at only forty-eight after a three year battle against cancer. They had been married for twenty-five years, and the only time spent apart during that time was the two years John served in Vietnam with the US Marine Corps.

John's apartment on Hawthorne Street was ideally located near to Prospect Park, the Botanic Gardens and the Brooklyn Museum. If he walked across Grand Army Plaza the Brooklyn Library was barely five minutes away. John spent much of most days, weather permitting, in the park, the museum, or the library.

One Sunday morning in late fall the weather was sunny and quite warm, so John decided to take a stroll through the park. There were few folks around at eight8 a.m., just a couple walking their dog. He stopped at the news-stand and bought the Sunday Times and made for a nearby bench where another guy of about his age was reading his paper. John sat and looked out over the scene across the lake towards the bridge on the other side, the low sun glistening on the water and the beautiful variety of trees. He took a deep lungful of fresh air, then turned to the guy next to him,

"Great day again."

The other man folded his paper and smiled, nodding in agreement. He was slim built, taller than John, well over six feet he guessed, with a short trimmed beard.

"Hi. Yes, indeed. Really beautiful." He extended his hand to John. "George Tyler. Good to meet you."

John shook George's hand warmly. Makes a change to speak to someone, he thought.

"John Swanson. Do you live nearby? I'm on Hawthorne Street."

Yes, it did feel good to have some kind of conversation with another human being. Much better than looking out the apartment window or yelling at the TV.

"Not near. No," replied George. "South Plainfield an hour west of here. You know it?"

"Heard of it but never been there."

George smiled and continued, "I've been coming here nearly twenty years now. There's so much to see within easy walking distance, and, of course, here in the park in good weather like today. It's just too good to miss."

"I couldn't agree more George. Amazing we never met until today. I guess we must have always been passing in opposite directions! I'm so pleased we met. It's good to have someone to talk to don't you think?"

George threw his head back and laughed, then slapped John on the back. "Yeah. That is incredible. I'm sick and tired of talking to myself. You alone like me?"

John looked down, serious for a moment.

"Yes. I lost my wife Kate fifteen years ago, and I never see my sons, daughter or grandkids these days. So apart from here, the library is my refuge."

"What a coincidence John. I've been on my own for fifteen years, same as you."

"Do you think perhaps we could arrange to meet another time George? Maybe have a beer?"

George was warming to the conversation, "Great. I'd like that. Look, here's my number." George tore a page from his pocket notebook and scribbled his number. "I'll be here again tomorrow, or maybe we could meet at Farrell's Bar and Grill and have a bite to eat? You know it?"

"Yes of course. And here, have my card as well. The number's on there. See you at Farrell's at, say, midday tomorrow George?"

They stood, shook hands, then walked off in opposite directions, and after about twenty yards they both turned and saluted goodbye. The same couple with the dog strolled by again.

The following day they met at Farrell's just before twelve, ordered beer, chili and fries, then found a table near the window. It didn't take long to discover they had lots in common apart from losing their wives in the same year. John, a former marine, learned that George had been a Seabee with the Naval Construction Force (NCF) and that they had served in Vietnam at the same time 68 through early '70.

"So tell me George. Where were you based in 'Nam?"

"Mainly at Khe Sanh, John. You?"

"I should have guessed it would be another coincidence, I was too! First Battalion, Colonel Padley's 26th Marines. Most of the time at base, but I had two short spells at the Hill 881 outpost."

"Hell, this is unbelievable. We dropped acoustic sensors around the 881 perimeter. I bet you were there John. Unless of course like now we were passing in opposite directions!"

There was indeed a never-ending list of things the two men had in common, and outside at gone three pm they agreed to meet again at the same time on the following Sunday.

On Sunday John waited expectantly at Farrell's, and it was nearly half past twelve by the time he had finished his first beer before George rushed in through the door looking all hot and out of breath. They shook hands and sat down,

"What the hell happened to you George? Stay there and catch your wind while I get you a beer."

George seemed to have gathered his breath by the time John returned from the bar,

"Now tell me George, what's the hurry? You really have to take things much slower at our age you know. Here, have a look at the menu and we'll order some chow. Pasta, or if you're really hungry I find the steak is always very good in here."

Taking his time studying the menu George explained, "Well, you know how it is John. My daughter and kids came over this morning early, so that made me late for the train."

John took a long swig from his beer, then put his head down, looking into the glass for a couple of minutes. If there was one thing that upset him these days, it was talk about children. Then he looked up at George,

"Not so sure how that feels. You're so lucky. We had four children and I now have seven grandkids. Never see them. Never see much of anyone other than passers-by on the street. Being on your own all the time makes you feel pretty isolated. But then hopefully you'll never know quite how that feels with family and grandkids nearby."

"Aw that's too bad John. Yours live overseas or out West? You're so right. I am very lucky."

"My eldest son lives and works in London; another is based in Houston. One daughter in San Francisco, she's not married, and then my youngest daughter, Samantha, lives out at Roslyn, so no more than an hour away on the Long Island Rail Road."

"Does the one nearest, in Roslyn, have kids?"

"Yes, George. Just the one. David's his name. He must be about seven by now. They're always too busy, you know. I guess we sometimes forget how we were at the same age. What with work, small kids at school, the struggle to pay the mortgage each month, and as for health insurance! They have to get on with their busy lives but it would be nice now and again to see the grandkids. I miss out not being the hands on grandpa. You know just occasionally, I'd love to take David to the fairground, play ball in the park, or take in a movie. That would give me back a real purpose in life. All kids should have a grandpa. Don't you think George? "

"I agree with you there, John. It would be good for you, and the grandkids could have so much fun. I know mine do."

George went for a well done steak and John chose a spaghetti carbonara. Over the meal the talk was mainly about family, and before they knew it, another two hours had passed.

George drained his beer and stood, "Sorry John, but have to fly. My next train to Plainfield is in fifteen minutes. Otherwise I'll miss evening Mass. I try to go every day."

John stood and they shook hands and gave each other a bear-like man-hug,

"Yeah. Great George. Let's do this again. Say this coming Wednesday?"

"I'll be here John."

The following Wednesday just after one pm, and George was becoming quite anxious, as John hadn't appeared. He tried his landline and cell phone but there was no answer. He left a message for John to call him, finished his beer and headed home.

A further month passed with no word from John, so George caught an early train into Brooklyn and went to the Hawthorne Street apartment block. There was no answer to John's buzzer so he tried the janitor who answered, "Can I help you?"

"Yes. I'm trying to contact Mr. John Swanson in apartment twnty-three?"

The janitor was a bit hesitant, "Can I ask who's speaking?"

"Yes. My name's George Tyler, I'm a friend of John's."

"Well, Mr Tyler, I'm sorry to say that Mr Swanson passed away three weeks ago. Do you know of any family? We have no knowledge of any relatives. We could only find evidence of his service in the Marines, and the Records Office in St. Louis wouldn't, or couldn't, say much family wise other than the service sheet shows only where he was born and the fact that he was married."

Apart from what little John had told him about his family, George had no details. "The only thing I do know is that he does have family and the nearest is a daughter who lives in Roslyn but I don't know her married name. Sorry."

A couple of minutes must have passed and George thought the janitor had cut off.

"Hello. Are you there?"

"Yes, Mr Tyler. I have to tell you that we had no choice but to rely on the city authorities to take over the arrangements for burial, as we had no knowledge of any family. He was interred only yesterday, on Hart Island."

"But surely that's the unmarked graveyard where no one can ever visit?"

George waited, and waited, his mind spinning with the implications of such dreadful news from the janitor. He cleared his throat and called, Hello? Hello? Are you there?"

There was no reply. Only silence at the other end of the apartment block intercom.

Terminus

George was deeply shocked by the news of John's sad ending, alone, and with no contact with family. It was as though this proud veteran, his good friend, had never existed. There was only one place to go and mull over what to do next, and ten minutes later he was back in Farrell's and sat at the same table he had last shared with John. Three beers later, and George reached the only decision he could in the circumstances. He determined that the least he could do in John's memory was to trace his daughter Samantha in Roslyn, no matter what the cost or how long it would take.

Back home in South Plainfield George made a coffee, sat at his desk and opened a fresh notebook, which would be dedicated to recording everything he knew about John and his family. It didn't take long:

- John Swanson age 65

- Born Texas, Amarillo

- Married to Kate - died aged 48

- Four children and seven grandkids. No contact details.

- Eldest son in London

- Other son Houston

- Daughter in San Francisco

- Nearest daughter Samantha in Roslyn, no surname known
- Samantha has boy David, age 7
- Marine served Khe Sanh 1968/70
- Lived Brooklyn 15 years

Exhausted he left the desk, slumped into the recliner and sank into a deep sleep.

The following days passed, then weeks; time seemed to fly by, and so preoccupied had George become with the task of searching for fresh information about John's family, that three months had passed with no luck in uncovering anything of use. Amongst the many avenues he pursued George had Googled the name Swanson in London, Houston, San Francisco, each resulting in   several names, none of which had any connection with John. He had also tried telephone directories and electoral registers but these simply confirmed the Google leads.

He knew from the conversation with the Hawthorne Street janitor that the Marines Records Office had nothing useful to add to what he already knew, so he called the Department for Veterans Affairs at their Brooklyn office and explained the circumstances of John's passing and that he had been buried in the potters field, Hart Island.

"My God, Mr Tyler, thanks you for letting us know. If only we had known we would have made sure he had a proper funeral fitting for a vet who had done so much for the nation."

"Yes I'm sure," George replied. "But I wasn't at all sure who else to get in touch with, as the Marine Records Office weren't able to help. Do you have any knowledge of his family?"

"I'm afraid not Mr Tyler. Have you tried the local newspaper office in Roslyn?"

"No I hadn't. Thank you I'll try them in the morning. Thanks for your help anyway." He was half way to replacing the handset assuming that's all the young lady had to say, "Mr. Tyler? Hello?"

"Yes. Yes. I'm here" he replied.

"There was just one thing you perhaps ought to know. We have on record that Mr. Swanson was awarded the Medal of Honor as well as the Purple Heart. He was a very highly decorated Marine."

"No I didn't know that. Thank you. In any case, he was a very modest man so would never have ever mentioned it."

The next day George called the offices of the Roslyn News and asked for their help in tracing Samantha. A reporter called Mike answered and listened carefully to the story behind his so far pretty fruitless efforts.

"Gee I'm sorry George. It's a fascinating story I'd love to follow through, but without a surname to go on, it's going to prove damned difficult."

"I understand. I just thought it would be worth a try." For the second time in two days George was about to hang up when Mike called out, "Wait! I just had a thought George. You said the daughter's name was Samantha and she has a boy of seven called David?"

"Yes that's right Mike."

"I think I overheard one of my colleagues talking about her friend at the gym called Sam. Look. Give me your number George, and I'll call you right back."

"Thank you, Mike. Much appreciated." George gave him the number then went to the kitchen to make fresh coffee.

It was an hour later that the phone rang. It was Mike from the News.

"George? George it's Mike in Roslyn." There seemed a sense of urgency in Mike's tone.

"Yes Mike. Any news?"

"My hunch paid off George!" Mike sounded excited. He continued, "Geri here in the office knows a Samantha Carter who has a boy called David! I think we found them George!"

The telephone rang in the Carter house. David rushed to answer as his mom was out back,

"The Carter household, David speaking. How can I help you?"

George hadn't expected David to answer, "Hi David. I really needed to speak to your mom."

David dropped the phone and ran out to the back yard calling, "Mom! Mom! I think it's Grandpa on the phone, can I talk to him? Please Mom. Please."

Sam came indoors. It had been some time since she last spoke to her dad.

"Hi, Dad. Good to hear you. It's been a while. How are you?"

This was going to be difficult. George took a deep breath, "Mrs Carter, Samantha? I'm sorry, my name is George Tyler, a friend of your father's." He then explained how he had come to know her dad and that they had become such firm friends. He then paused, taking another deep breath,

"I'm sorry to be the bearer of bad news, but your dad died over three months ago and I didn't know how to contact you until now."

"Oh no! How? When? What happened?"

George told her the whole story of how he discovered John had died, and where he had to be buried.

Samantha couldn't find words to reply for a full two minutes. Then, her voice much quieter, she put the handset closer to her ear, "My God. Not Hart Island surely? That's where all the street people, and down-and-outs go!"

"I'm so sorry, but there was no other way......," George replied.

Sam was speechless, went to the kitchen and sat quietly staring at the tabletop. David followed her, "Has Grandpa gone Mom? I wanted to speak to him. Mom why are you crying?"

Samantha held a tissue to her face and sobbed, heartbroken,

"Yes. Grandpa Swanson has gone honey. Gone to live with Jesus."

6

Pizza with Salad or Chips?

Dad was on great form and enjoying every moment, "You've made both Mum and I extremely happy today. We're so very proud of you."

Jane had done much better than everyone expected with a 2.2 in Media Studies. With the degree awards ceremony and also her twenty-second birthday, today was cause for a double celebration.

Two months earlier Professor Julian Cranshaw had addressed the undergraduates.

'Ladies and Gentlemen, you have today received your finals, and next month your parents will be present on the occasion of your graduation, also a truly proud moment for them I'm sure. This is the start of the rest of your life, as they say, and I have no doubt that your achievement will unlock the door to success in whatever career you choose to follow.'

At that point the professor had paused for a breath and his usual sip of water, although everyone was agreed that, to put it in Biblical terms, the water had turned to wine and was actually gin and tonic. He cleared his throat before continuing,

'Graduates from this university are in great demand not only throughout the United Kingdom and everywhere, world-wide. The exciting opportunities awaiting you, will I am sure, result in great success for you all in future. My most heartfelt congratulations to you all. Thank you, and well done.'

However life post-graduation was to prove quite the opposite of the inspiring speech given by Professor Cranshaw.

Once more living at home with her parents Peter and Anita, on weekdays Jane used Dad's desktop computer and printer whilst he was at work. Over the past twelve-plus months she had submitted over a hundred applications in response to advertised vacancies either directly or indirectly associated with media. The majority of her letters hadn't even been acknowledged.

Monday, the start of another week, and it was a particularly miserable day out, cold and blowing a virtual gale. Although not yet two in the afternoon Jane had already turned on the desk lamp. Mum came in from the kitchen and wrapped her arms round Jane's shoulders gave her a big hug and whispered,

"Don't worry, darling. It will all work out okay, you'll see. We must just be patient you know."

Pointing to the picture which had pride of place on Dad's desk, with a sigh she added, "To think your graduation photograph was taken over twelve months ago. Where has all that time gone?"

At home that evening the after supper conversation was mainly about Jane's work prospects. Anita's usual smiley demeanour was for once quite serious. "I thought it was very sad to see her this afternoon at your desk. No calls, and nothing in the post again today. I think she's losing heart. Poor girl seems really quite depressed. And she's such an attractive girl, I would also have thought that by now she would have lots of friends or even a special boyfriend. But she doesn't seem to have much of a social life since her graduation. "

Peter was deep in thought. He nodded, acknowledging Anita's concern. "Yes, I agree. Forgive me for being an old cynic, but you know I've always held the view that compared with my day the number of young people graduating from universities today must have grown at least tenfold. Certainly the number of new so-called universities established seems so far to have satisfied the demand for places. Makes the unemployment statistics for all young people under twenty-five look not so bad I suppose."

He hesitated before continuing, "You know it makes me wonder what chance have all these young people got. Perhaps they would be better off leaving school at sixteen and going straight to work. At least that way they'll be gaining work experience. Shame they did away with National Service I say."

The sombre Anita had listened attentively to Peter's thoughts on the matter. It wasn't the first time she'd heard it. "I do agree with you, but surely the problem at the end of the day is that there just aren't enough jobs to meet the needs of all these out –of-work youngsters?"

At the next Job Centre appointment Helen, the advisor Jane had seen previously, had what she obviously felt was the very news her client had been waiting for. "Well, Jane, there's very little new to report since last I saw you; however, did you know that Waitrose are opening a new giant superstore in Wembley? They need large numbers of floor staff as well as till work. Although it probably means shift work at least they pay more than Job Seekers Allowance. I see that they offer an attractive package, with staff discounts, two weeks' paid holiday, pay if you're off sick, and double time for working on bank holidays."

With the usual look of disappointment, now quite despairing of ever finding a proper job, Jane was on the verge of tears. "So, it appears that the only work open to me are jobs working in a restaurant or a supermarket. I obviously wasted my time for three years at university and my degree is proving to be quite worthless. I do find it all pretty depressing."

Helen smiled, but had nothing further to say on the matter; after all, she did have a job, and one she enjoyed.

Peter and Anita had done more for Jane than she could have expected, so she vowed to find a way of making it up to them. As for repaying the tuition fees, it didn't look as though that was ever going to happen.

To allow sufficient time to continue with her job search, and in order to earn at least enough to cover the cost of her keep, Jane eventually submitted to the 'encouragement' from Helen at the Job Centre and took an evening job as a waitress at the Pizza Parlour in Granville Street. There she met three other graduates who had been similarly pressured into the work under the threat of losing Job Seekers Allowance. One of them, Karen, had been there for four years.

The parlour was owned by Mr Alexandros

Georgios, a jolly, bald, overweight man in his late fifties, married with six children. He was part of a large Greek family of restaurant owners in various parts of North London. Mr George as he was known, also had an interest in the Kostas Café owned by his brother Nick. The Kostas was no more than a five-minute walk away.

Work at the parlour was hard, but Jane enjoyed the company of the other girls, and generally speaking, most of the customers were very pleasant. They served a wide variety of pizza as well as the usual burger, salad, and chips, either to eat in or take away. Fully licensed, the profit was really made on the vastly inflated drinks prices. Often in the late evening Greek friends of Mr George would arrive, and still be there drinking when the staff finished clearing the tables and went home. Despite the long hours, Jane was at last earning money, and the tips were good.

After being there six months Peter asked how Jane felt things were going on the job front generally, and for the time being at the Pizza Parlour.

"Still nothing from all the applications I've sent Dad, and although things are okay for the time being at the parlour, I'm a little concerned that my late shifts seem to come around more frequently than the other girls. I don't think that's fair."

Forever protective of his daughter Peter looked quite shocked, "That's bad darling. You should take this up with Mr George, and if you don't get anywhere, I'll be having a word with that gentleman."

"I will Dad, thanks."

It wasn't worth mentioning, and might just be coincidence, but Jane had noticed that when she was on the late shift, the regular chef was invariably replaced in the kitchen by Yannis who also worked daytimes at the Kostas. She gathered from the other girls that when they were on lates, Mr George's daughter Adrienne was always doing the cooking.

On a quiet Tuesday evening in late November, Mr George wasn't in. So Jane decided to confide in her friend Karen who sat, held her hand, and smiled reassuringly, "You've been here all this time and he hasn't come on to you yet?"

"No," Jane replied

"Oh, he will. He does with all the girls. Dirty old man."

The following Friday evening it was exceptionally busy, and a few times as she was winding her way from the kitchen and round the tables, Jane could swear something or someone lightly touched her bottom. Mr George stood to one side of the kitchen door, and later as she came through from the kitchen he winked at her, "I must say, Jane, you are looking quite ravishing this evening, lovely."

Smiling, he reached out and ran his hand down her thigh, at the same time bending forward as if to kiss her. Jane recoiled in horror. How dare this middle-aged fat man touch her so intimately?

"Mr George, no!"

Shocked, she turned and busied herself cleaning and tidying the tables furthest from the kitchen. The other waitress must have sensed what had happened and while Jane continued to take the last customer orders Carla took them from her and brought the food from the kitchen to the tables. Absolutely fuming, and finding it hard to hold back the tears, Jane was not going to let him get away with it, the others might accept it but not her, never. The more she thought about it the angrier she became. At closing time she stormed out without a word, and on her way home she kept thinking what on earth would her dad say if she told him what had happened.

At 1.30 am the following morning Adrienne, who was the named key-holder, received a call at home that the restaurant fire alarm had triggered and was disturbing nearby homes. It must have been no more than ten minutes when she arrived at the parlour. The noise from the alarm was deafening. No wonder it had woken everyone in the neighbourhood. Adrienne unlocked the door, turned the alarm off and the lights on. She was choking so badly she felt as though the coughing would cause her to be sick. She held a handkerchief to her mouth, the stench of burning was overpowering. The smoke was coming from the kitchen. When she opened the door Adrienne took one look and let out the most terrified scream

"Ohhh noooooooooooooo."

Mr George, her father, was hanging head and shoulders into the deep fat fryer, which was still on. He'd most definitely had his chips, but tonight no salad.

7

Still Seeking the Meaning of Life
(The RAOB Mystery)

Edward had now been working at the Gazette office for over six months since starting work in January 1950, just before his fifteenth birthday, and there were still lots of things he was struggling to understand better. 'Forever curious, and blessed with a vivid imagination' was how the Headmaster at school had once described him.

Every Monday morning his first job was to call on the cemetery Superintendent, Mr Morgan, to check details of any new customers reported during the past weekend. Interesting that. thought Edward, because he had learned a great deal about the world of work in the past six months; for example, back in the office Mr Mosby, Mr Barraclough and Tracy, each had two wire trays on their desk, one marked

'IN' and the other labelled 'OUT', whereas the Superintendent's desk had only one tray. Also, last Thursday evening Edward had asked Dad why Mr B referred to Mr Morgan as 'Digger', and Dad replied with a smile and a wink, "That's because he's Australian son".

Once a month the second Monday morning call was to a semi-detached house in Worthing, 18 Aldwick Street. Edward had never met the person who lived there, but his job was simply to collect an envelope marked RAOB, which was always drawing pinned to the shed door. On his return to the office with the monthly RAOB envelope, Mr Mosby insisted on opening it personally, explaining that it contained information that only he was allowed to know about. He said it was something to do with the 'Buffs'. However, after by the end of March Edward was at least allowed to know that the envelope contained a notice of the next meeting of the Buffs, but he was none the wiser as to what it all meant.

Every month, the same routine, and Edward wondered why the occupant of 18 Aldwick Street was always out. He found this very strange. It never occurred to him that whoever lived there might actually be at work whenever he called. No. He was convinced this had to be something quite sinister, and he was determined to find out more about the mystery surrounding the RAOB.

At home on Monday evening Edward went to bed early and studied the dictionary looking to find more information about either the Buffs or RAOB, but found nothing. What was all this secrecy about, and why was it that there were so many things adults knew about that apparently weren't suitable subjects for younger people, assuming they wouldn't understand. It all seemed so unfair, after all he was fifteen.

The following day Edward went across the road to the library. In the entrance he was confronted by Mrs Stevenson, the next-door neighbour, "Hello Edward. And how can I help you today?"

This was most unexpected. Why hadn't Mum ever mentioned that Mrs Stevenson worked at the library? What would she think if he asked where to find information about the RAOB?

"Er… mmmm…, hello, Mrs Stevenson. Is there a section for reference books?"

"Yes Edward. On the first floor."

Edward spent the next hour scouring the books in the reference section, and eventually he found what he had been looking for. Under the heading 'the Royal Antediluvian Order of the Buffaloes', the footnote included the remarks "in the early nineteenth century, secret societies were looked upon as potentially being dangerous and subversive."

"That's it!" he called out. The other readers stopped and stared disapprovingly. Edward mouthed an 'I'm sorry' and quietly returned to the open book which told him everything he needed to know on the matter, 'secret society, dangerous, subversive, antediluvian, – whatever that meant.' This was something he couldn't, perhaps shouldn't, even tell Dad about. Best just to say nothing, he decided. It was only six months after starting work and he had already concluded that the world was indeed full of people involved in some very strange goings-on.

What further mysteries of life would be revealed by the time he was sixteen he wondered?

8

Elvis Lives
(near Doncaster)

Albert was in the front room and studying a page in his book '10 Most Evocative Elvis Lyrics'. He sat at the piano singing along as he read.

Redundancy

Apart from the day he married Enid, the other two unforgettable events in the life of Albert Swithenbank were 16th August 1977, the day Elvis died, and 26th November 1993 when the pit closed, resulting in almost every other man in the village being made redundant, including Albert.

At the age of fifty-six, and having worked as a coal miner from the age of fifteen, he was at a complete loss as to what to do next. Albert felt worthless, and, without work, somehow less of a man.

With the redundancy money in the bank, for the first time in their married life they could afford a holiday abroad and spent the whole of May on an all-inclusive package at the Costa Gran in Tenerife. With the climate, the food, the people, the entertainment, they both agreed this was their best holiday ever. Especially when compared with the usual annual week in a caravan at Cleethorpes.

Awakening

By November they had settled into a daily routine which never varied and as usual at half past twelve they sat down at the kitchen table for dinner. These days there was little in the way of conversation other than an occasional 'thanks love.' Enid felt that since Albert had been out of work, she had become just the housekeeper, and most of the time invisible.

She put the plate in front of Albert. He sat staring at his plate, deep in thought, although God only knows what about. After what must have been at least five minutes she broke the silence, "Albert?"

Albert looked up from his plate, "What is it Enid? You all right?"

"I'm fine," Enid smiled to re-assure him, then continued,

"I've been thinking. Other than the pit, the only

other thing you really know about is Elvis. You know everything there is about his life and his music."

"True, true," Albert replied. He only ever engaged in any meaningful discussion when the subject was Elvis.

Enid had indeed been thinking a lot recently, and now she couldn't hold back any longer, "Do you remember Hugh Rathbone, the Elvis impersonator at the Costa?"

Albert was now paying more attention to what she was saying, "Aye, I remember him. Pretty good, I thought, except that he didn't look right. Can't have been more than five eight."

"Yes, love. Well, I've heard you sing, and you're good. Only this morning I was bringing your tea from the kitchen and all I could hear was Elvis singing, at least I could swear it was one of his records. But when I opened the door it was just you. You're six feet tall the same as Elvis, and about the same weight, maybe a bit heavier, and other than your bald head, with an Elvis wig you could be much better than Hugh. And you'd look the part."

For the first time in months, Albert couldn't help smiling. Enid had definitely hit the right spot.

Elvis Lives

Three months later, and Albert had been transformed into the most realistic Elvis impersonator ever seen in South Yorkshire. White fringed jump suit, white studded leather belt, Elvis wig complete with sideburns, dark glasses and two-inch Cubans, size eleven the same as Elvis, even though Albert's real shoe size was nine.

Enid contacted all the Yorkshire concert secretaries websites and placed an ad for 'the newest and best ever Elvis impersonator' which resulted in three bookings in the first month. Her brother Cyril was employed at gigs as chauffeur, bodyguard and 'musical director' (he operated the backing tracks equipment).

For Albert as the reincarnated Elvis, life changed almost overnight with bookings nearly every weekend. At a time in life when most men had accepted a quiet retirement, he was as active as ever. The Bharat Social Club in Bradford was his favourite gig, particularly as the concert secretary Mr Sengupta, always paid the normal £50 appearance fee in cash, and occasionally included an extra tenner.

Trip to York

Just before Easter Enid went to stay with her sister Margaret in York for a couple of days. They really enjoyed their time together and Margaret felt much better for seeing Enid. However the time seemed to fly by and before they knew it they were sharing hugs and tears of goodbye before Enid boarded the train.

It had gone ten o'clock when the taxi pulled up outside 32 Empire Street. How times had changed, when nowadays she could afford to pay twenty quid for a taxi from Doncaster!

Enid was curious to see how Albert had managed without her while she was away. She unlocked the front door, stepped into the hallway and switched the light on. Somehow the house seemed different. Cold, with that strange musty dampness she had smelled so often before in buildings that had been empty for some time. She called out, "Albert? Are you there?" There was no reply.

Enid took the pile of mail from the doormat and went through to the kitchen to put the kettle on. One of the letters was from Phil Collinson at Granada Television. Phil was a Coronation Street producer and apparently he wanted to meet Albert to discuss a possible appearance as the background entertainer for a wedding reception due to be filmed in May. Surely Albert hadn't been away for the past three days and missed out on this chance of playing in Corrie?

She took her case and tea upstairs, and on checking the wardrobe she saw that all Albert's clothes were still on their hangers. That is, except for his white jump suit, the white leather belt and boots with the two-inch Cubans. So perhaps he was just away at a gig? But for three days? Enid called Cyril, but he hadn't seen or heard from Albert either.

She didn't sleep that night, and the following morning she called the South Kirkby police in White Apron Street to report Albert missing.

Before dinner time two police constables arrived. She explained about her trip to Margaret's in York and her return the previous night to find the house deserted.

The older of the two PCs asked all the questions while the other took notes. "I understand Mrs Swithenbank, you did the right thing to call us. Can you think of where he might have gone? To family or friends? Do you have a photograph of your husband?"

Enid went to the sideboard and handed the constable a framed picture, "Yes, of course. Here's one taken at the Bharat Social Club in Bradford on Valentine's night."

Terminus

By the end of June and with no further trace of the missing Albert/Elvis, Enid had almost given up hope. Then unexpectedly the police station called and asked if she would go in as they had some news.

At the station DI Johnson showed her into an interview room and offered her a chair.

Enid leaned forward, "You've got some news then, Mr. Johnson?"

"Yes Mrs Swithenbank. We received a report from the police in Tenerife that we all believed might help with the investigation to trace your husband. We agreed with them that it would be worthwhile revisiting the case, starting at the Costa Gran Hotel again. This led them to the home of a Maria Hernandez, the former wife of Hugh Rathbone, who I think you may have known? For many years he used to be the resident entertainer at the hotel, until two years ago."

This was all getting too much for Enid, all too upsetting. The WPC handed her a box of tissues. Enid stared down at her lap and wiped tears from her eyes, "Please. Please tell me."

DI Johnson was also finding this difficult. He turned again to the open file on the table, "The police found a body hidden under the floorboards in the Hernandez apartment, which had been empty for some time. They also found clothes in a wardrobe which would have been worn by an Elvis impersonator and it was assumed they must have belonged to Mr Rathbone. I'm sorry Mrs Swithenbank, we can only conclude it's not Albert. There's no further action we can take at this time."

Enid was stunned. They were closing the file! Head bent, she sobbed, heartbroken. Had all this just been a waste of time? "But... but that can't be it, surely? Tell me, was there also a pair of white boots with Cuban heels?"

The DI looked back at the report, "Yes. Size eleven. With two-inch Cuban heels. What I thought strange at first is that the post-mortem says the person who died had feet probably smaller than size eleven. Nevertheless, it does say that identification was difficult. I'm sorry."

"Albert wore size eleven the same as Elvis. Believe me, Inspector it is him. Albert was actually a size nine."

Crying openly with relief that no matter what the police thought, she knew now that Albert was dead, and at the same time being shocked by the realization that he had most probably been having an affair with Maria Hernandez, in Tenerife!

Sobbing, she stood and turned towards the door, quietly acknowledging DI Johnson and the WPC,

"Thank you. Now I know. No matter what happened, I still loved him, and will always treasure his memory."

9

The Book Shop

"**M**anchester, Went there, once," said Grandad as he poked his pipe with his penknife, then started puffing again even though he'd run out of tobacco first thing after breakfast.

"Never stops " - inhaling deeply, followed by the usual fit of coughing, he spit into the open fire, followed by another spate of coughing, - "damned raining. Well known for it."

I still remember, he'd smiled, then turned to me, waving his pipe in the air, "Did you know that lad?"

I loved my grandad because he knew just about everything there was to know in the whole wide world. He'd even been as far as London, once.

Forty years later and here I was, thinking back to when I was twelve, and I still clearly remembered every one of grandad's stories.

Tonight was typical for an early December in Manchester. It was bitterly cold, and raining, with the occasional gust of wind which left me gasping for breath. It had been dark since four o'clock, and the poor street lighting made for a bloody miserable walk home along Brown Street. These new shoes weren't waterproof either; my feet were absolutely sodden. It had been a long day, and I was feeling pretty sorry for myself. Soaked through to the skin, tired and hungry, all I could think of was getting indoors, out of my wet clothes and into a hot bath. That was if the bathroom was free.

Home I called it! What kind of home was one room in a house shared with three others : two ancient monuments who never seemed to leave their rooms, although they probably did when I was out at work; and one gay bloke, Nigel Long, who was always telling me about 'going clubbing' with his friends. What kind of home was it for a man of fifty-two, widowed these past seven years, I hardly ever saw the children anymore. They all lived down South.

Brown Street was deserted, and the only sounds were the hissing rain, and my feet squelching through the ever deepening pools along the pavement. All the shops have been closed for hours. Normally at this time of night I would have expected to see lots of folk in the street on their way to the Eagle and Child, then later on to Barnaby's Club next door which was open until two. I wondered if it was one of the clubs Nigel went to?

It was just after ten as I was passing Chadwick's book shop. Odd, I thought, for the lights to be on at this time of night. I tried the door and much to my surprise it opened. I went in. The shop was in the old part of Brown Street where all the buildings are Grade II listed. The Chadwick family had run the business over the past hundred or so years. Other than the books, the inside of the shop hadn't probably changed much during that time. It wouldn't have seemed out of place in a Charles Dickens novel.

The shop looked empty. No customers, nor any sign of Mr Chadwick. At least it was warm and dry. I made my way to the fiction section and browsed through the book spines in the 'New Arrivals' section. There was a new John Grisham that looked interesting so I pulled it out and read the bio on the back sleeve. As I opened the book at the first page I sensed that maybe I wasn't alone after all, as my attention was drawn to a conversation between two men sat in the reading area towards the back of the shop. I could just see them through a gap in the shelving. The elder of the two was in his late eighties at least, I'd say, well over six feet tall, a hollow-cheeked gaunt man with long white hair back and sides, bald on top, and with saucer-like eyes looking as though permanently surprised. The younger man was aged about forty, much shorter, overweight, with dark brown hair greying round the ears. Both seemed unaware of my presence.

I gathered from the gist of their conversation they were studying a book on the history of the Boer War in South Africa. I began to listen more closely. The old man mumbled something about the author as though everyone should be familiar with his work.

"I take it you're a student of history?" The younger man nodded.

"Interesting you should choose that particular work, as it contains a great deal about my Father, Sir Alfred Milner. I'm Charles Milner by the way." With a smile, the old man extended his hand.

"Tim Chadwick. How do you do?" the younger man replied.

"Good to meet you Tim. I knew your great-grandfather well. We were at Levenshulme Grammar together. My father was in South Africa with the 6th Dragoon Guards, which is why I'm particularly interested to see you have this in stock."

My mind was in a whirl, thinking that this just can't be right; something just didn't stack up. To have been at grammar school with Tim's great- grandfather, the old man had to be at least 120 years old! I turned my attention back to the conversation, but now the voices were gradually tailing off, becoming quite faint. My God! I looked and there was no one in the reading area, just two chairs and a book on the table. Had this all just been some kind of dream? Was I hallucinating, or did this happen for real? What on earth was I doing in Chadwick's gone eleven o'clock on a Tuesday night? I put the Grisham back on the shelf and went to leave the empty shop.

Once outside I was relieved to see that the rain had stopped. I stood for a moment at the edge of the pavement, turned, and looked back. Chadwick's was in total darkness.

The following morning I was an hour late into the office and thankfully no one other than Keith had noticed. "Hi John. They're all off to a meeting in Preston this morning so it should be pretty quiet today."

Keith leaned back in his chair, swung his feet up onto the desk, and opened up this week's Middleton and North Manchester Gazette.

"It sounds as though you're starting with a cold John."

"Yes Keith. Got a real soaking last night," I replied.

"Have you seen the paper? It's got a story about the owner of that book shop in Brown Street.

You know the one, Chadwick's?"

"Yes I know it. What's that about? I was" –
Keith started to read before I could finish. "The
inquest concluded on Tuesday into the sudden and
unexplained death on 17th August last, of book shop
owner Mr Timothy Chadwick, aged forty two. The
coroner returned an open verdict."

Keith folded the paper, "More to that than meets
the eye I wouldn't mind betting."

This was so unreal, I thought, really spooky,
dream-like. Surely I couldn't have imagined it all?

"But, Keith, I saw him when I was in Chadwick's
only last night. Yet the paper says he died in August?"

The phone rang, "Keith Bradshaw. How can I
help you today?"

10

Heads Up

Performance Appraisal

It was three years since Jane took up her first teaching post at St Barnabas First School, and time once more for her annual appraisal interview with Head Eileen Hart. These interviews were invariably conducted face to face, seated in the very comfortable leather armchairs. They had already discussed the detailed assessments all of which were marked either 'Satisfactory' or 'Exceeds Expectations',

"So Jane, to sum up, another very successful year. I couldn't have asked more of you since you first came to St Barnabas. The staff, the children, and parents all speak so highly of you, and I know that also goes for most of the governors."

Eileen turned the appraisal form over to the

back page summary. She looked up at Jane, and it was hard to tell which of them had the broadest smile, "Even though three years' experience is relatively early in your career it gives me great pleasure to tell you that my recommendation is…" Eileen cleared her throat, adjusted her glasses, and read the briefest of comments,

"Outstanding. Deputy and Head material for the future."

"Thank you so much Eileen. I'm very happy here, and I love the children. Your report is much more than I could ever have expected, although the thought of taking on further responsibility is something I hadn't even considered. Thank you again for all you've done for me."

They both stood and shook hands; then Eileen returned to her desk. As Jane headed for the door, Eileen called after her, "There's just one thing before you go."

"Yes, Eileen?"

"We break for the summer tomorrow, and immediately on your return in September, I want you to take over Class M3 from Albert. He'll be helping me prepare for the bishop's visit and then the OFSTED inspection which both come before the end of the month."

Jane was quite taken aback by this news. She had become very fond of the children in M2, "Well, this is an unexpected turn of events Eileen! But what about my current class until Albert is free from helping you?"

"I'm putting in a supply until after the inspection; then Albert will take over until the summer holiday."

Jane's mind was in a spin. A change at the last moment before half-term was the last thing she wanted, and Albert of all people!

It was as if Eileen could read her thoughts, "I can guess how you feel Jane, but this inspection is particularly important. Of course on the plus side your children now in M2 will be moving up after the summer so you'll have them back under your wing for the rest of the year." Above all, Eileen was keen to keep Jane on-side.

"Yes. I hadn't thought of that" Jane replied.

"I'll leave it to you to break the news to the children. But do reassure them it's only temporary and that they will be with you again after the hols. One last thing if you don't mind. Ask Kate on the way out to give you the file of Albert's last reports on the children in M3. If I can suggest you study them and get some kind of feel for their current progress."

"I'll do that Eileen, thanks Of course it's not as though they don't know me already as I take them for RE once a week."

Jane left the head's office still trying to make sense of this sudden change. Kate wasn't in the outer office so she would have to come back later.

Albert Humphries

Albert was Eileen's deputy and he was the only person at St Barnabas Jane wasn't overly fond of; in she fact positively disliked him. He was a short balloon-shaped man originally from Swansea. Many in the staff room often described his facial expression as having the appearance of being permanently angry about something. This view was echoed by Jane's closest friend Kate Williams, the head's PA, who said that he always looked as though he 'hated his fellow teachers, people in general, and probably quite dislikes himself.' To state the obvious he was not universally popular among both staff and children.

After lunch Jane went to see Kate to ask for the file of reports on Class M3,

"Hi Jane. I know what you're after. Eileen told me." Kate opened the filing cabinet,

"Now. Let me see..." Leafing through the pockets for a second time her frown deepened then turning to Jane she sighed,

"I don't understand, that's strange. It was definitely there this morning and no one else has asked for it. Where could that damned file have gone?"

Jane stood as if to leave, "Not to worry, Kate, I'm sure it'll turn up. It would have been nice to be able to read the reports during the break, but I'm sure everything will work out okay. By the way, you haven't forgotten our date for drinks tonight?"

"No, I hadn't forgotten. Looking forward to it. I'll see you in there around seven?"

"Seven o'clock it is then. I'll try to be there a little earlier if I can."

Jane arrived in the Rose and Crown in Montague Street at a quarter to seven. The place was full of character and had a great atmosphere, ideal for chatting over a meal. They always sat at the same table near the window overlooked by the low oak beam carrying the message 'RELAX YOU HAVE NOW LEFT THE RAT RACE,' which had no particular significance other than they both found it amusing.

It was quite busy and there was a queue at the bar in the restaurant area. Jane joined in at the end next to the fish tank, and as she waited there was a tap on her shoulder, it was Kate,

"Need some company?"

"Ah. You made it darling. What will you have?"

"Chardonnay as usual if you don't mind Jane. I'll go to the table before anyone else takes it."

It wasn't long before Jane was served and she was quickly sat alongside Kate. They exchanged a two-cheek peck, touched glasses with the usual 'cheers'. They chatted about their plans for the holidays – Kate's holiday in the States and Jane's new flat; then the subject switched to the move to M3 in September, and the fact that Albert had recently been quite abrupt whenever he met Jane, or simply ignored her. He was so rude.

Kate sipped her wine, taking her time before continuing, "If you ask me, he's got one helluva big chip on his shoulder about his height. Probably due to the fact that all the other staff are all taller than him, and the way the children are shooting up these days, it won't be long before some of them will tower above him as well. I'm sure Eileen's not too fond of him either."

Jane nodded in agreement, "That's the impression I get as well."

"Between these four walls, I can tell you that the last time Albert was standing in for Eileen I came in from tea in the staff room and he was looking at your personal file. He looked so angry, slammed the file on the desk and stormed out. I think he bears quite a grudge against you for some reason. Be careful Jane is my advice, I don't trust him."

"How strange, Kate. I've never done anything to cause him any offence."

"Of course not. You made your mark here from the day you arrived, and I know that Eileen thinks very highly of you. If Albert left you'd be a very popular choice as deputy head if you ask me."

Eileen is Feeling Unwell

By the end of September, the visits by the bishop and OFSTED had taken place and were considered to have been very successful. The school inspection resulted in an outstanding assessment, much better than expected. On both counts, Eileen's plan to make the most of Albert's support had certainly been justified.

On the Monday morning following receipt of the OFSTED report, Jane arrived early and went straight to her classroom to check over her teaching plan before assembly. She opened the table drawer, and to her surprise there was the file of the missing reports on M3! Forget all the mystery about where the file had been all these weeks, Jane had a pretty good idea, where and who was behind it.

That evening Jane met Kate in the Rose and Crown for supper. The topic of conversation, however, was not at all about Kate's holiday in Florida, or Jane's flat move. Kate just didn't seem her usual cheery self, "I couldn't say anything earlier but I'm worried about Eileen."

Jane seemed surprised, "Why, Kate? Is there something wrong? I saw her a few times during August and she seemed okay to me."

Kate emptied her glass before continuing, "When I got back from the States a week ago, I picked up a message from her asking me to pop round to see her. Anyway, apparently in the past couple of weeks she'd been feeling unwell, and complained of recurring headaches, dizziness and palpitations. She's had an upset tummy and been sick a couple of times."

They sat quietly for a couple of minutes, then Kate turned to Jane and took her hand, "Poor Eileen. I think she should see a doctor but she's very reluctant to go, you know how she is."

"Yes, I agree, Kate. We must do whatever it takes and watch her carefully." Jane replied.

The news of Eileen's ill health virtually killed off the rest of the conversation. So, having eaten their meal in silence, they left by nine thirty.

Worthing Accident & Emergency

On Friday morning Kate arrived for work unusually late, after assembly. She hung her coat up then knocked on Eileen's door to offer her apologies. She was horrified to see her boss collapsed at the desk, with her arms outstretched and head on the desk.

Kate rushed to her side, bent closely to look at her face and gently shook her shoulder, "Oh God. No. Eileen can you hear me?"

After a few moments Eileen moved, then very slowly she sat upright as though waking from a sleep. Her eyes were glazed and her face drooped looking just as though she'd suffered a stroke, the same as in the TV advert,

"I'll be okay, just need a moment…" Her speech was slurred,

"Oh no you're not. I'm calling an ambulance. Don't move."

Having arrived at Worthing Hospital, the next five hours were taken up with blood tests, and a thorough physical examination by both the on-duty A & E doctor then the consultant, and they were unable to pin down exactly what was wrong with Eileen. The dizzy spells now came with alarming regularity and the severe headache never left her. Three times in the next couple of hours she was violently sick and her condition had deteriorated dramatically since first feeling unwell earlier that morning. She was really very poorly, and was transferred to the Medical Assessment Unit in the late afternoon.

The actual cause of Eileen's illness was puzzling the doctors as all the test results indicated that she had not had a stroke. That evening Jane rang Kate to find out how Eileen was getting on, "Hi, Kate. How are you? Any news?"

"I'm fine thanks. Just a little tired. Eileen's still in the MAU and I understand she's showing signs of improvement, so perhaps she may be allowed home tomorrow."

Jane was anxious to know more, "But surely

something is causing her to be so ill. Do they really have no idea?"

"Well, the hospital puts it largely down to stress. When she's well enough to be discharged, they have advised two weeks complete rest. I don't quite know what to do Jane."

The following Tuesday morning, Kate went to each classroom in turn with a note from the LEA. The note was brief and to the point:

'Sadly Eileen, our head, is unwell at the moment and she has been advised to take two weeks sick leave. Whilst she's away Mr Jack Gregory from St Joseph's will be covering the head's duties on a temporary basis.'

As far as Albert was concerned the message was all too clear. Someone, presumably Kate, had informed the Authority. He hadn't been consulted or involved at all.

Within days of Jack's arrival, Albert made it known that he had applied for another post and hoped to return to Wales. Needless to say, the news of Albert's probable departure from St Barnabas was a matter of considerable relief for both staff and children.

Goodbye

Eileen intended to return to work and had called Jane during the weekend to ask if they could have a chat in her office at eight o'clock on the Monday morning,

"Sorry to sound a bit secretive Jane but I wanted to have a private chat with you before anyone else arrives. I really called to let you know that lots of things have been happening in the background during my absence, and in the end I've had to come to terms with the fact that I'm not going to improve sufficiently to carry on as before. I'm still having the headaches and upset tummy; it's almost like being poisoned. So, it's now been confirmed that I will be taking early retirement. For the moment this is only between you and I, Jane. There will be no formal announcement before Friday. Anyway, you should watch developments next week when I guess there will be an ad in both the TES and Catholic Teachers Gazette. You must apply, Jane. I think the majority of the school governors are likely to favour you when the time comes."

"My God, Eileen. How very sad it's come to this. But your health is the most important thing. And of course you can be assured that this is strictly between us and goes no further than this room."

Only a few weeks earlier, and Albert would have assumed that he would replace Eileen, and it would have been equally obvious to all except Albert that he was never going to get the job. He was just too unpopular, narcissistic and generally unpleasant in his dealings with both staff and pupils. Even the lollipop lady at the school crossing disliked him intensely.

The following week Eileen's impending vacancy was advertised, and Jane applied. Barely a week after submitting the application, Terry Spencer, the chair of governors, asked to see her. It was meant to be an informal approach so he saw Jane at home.

Having made themselves comfortable with coffee they chatted about the events surrounding Eileen's ill health over the past months and were agreed what a great loss to the school her retirement would be. Terry then turned to what was obviously the purpose of his call.

"On behalf of the governors I must say Jane, how pleased we are that you have applied to fill the vacancy. We found your CV very interesting and I know that Eileen has always spoken very highly of you."

"I don't know what to say, Mr Spencer. Thank you. I'm really quite humbled by your faith in me and regardless of the outcome I will be forever grateful to Eileen."

Terry had finished and stood to leave, "That's a lovely plant you have there, Jane. I'm sure I've seen it before in somewhere before but haven't known it indoors. Might have been on a visit to Kew."

Jane smiled, always pleased to show her knowledge of rare plants, "Yes. I brought it from my father's greenhouse when they moved. He is quite the expert. It's commonly known as the desert rose. It's found almost everywhere in East Africa, but because it needs lots of sunlight, in our climate it's best kept indoors. It has to be handled with great care, as the roots and stem are extremely toxic. If ingested, the sap can cause severe headaches, dizzy spells and nausea. For animals and humans alike it's potentially fatal. Nevertheless, I agree, it really is a beautiful plant."

Welcome

A month later, and the newly appointed head of St Barnabas First School was in early. There was a knock on the door and Kate popped her head in with the widest smile ever,

"Morning, Head."

Jane looked up from her desk, "Morning again Kate. Thank you so much for the support you've given me over the past six months."

Kate nodded and turned as if to go back to the outer office. Jane stared out of the window, her back to Kate, deep in thought…

"All these long months... Albert's gone, dear Eileen's gone, and despite all the drama, in the end it couldn't have worked out better don't you think?"

Kate smiled knowingly but didn't say anything. She closed the door and returned to her desk.

11

Online Dating

Online dating sites appeal to so many because of the relative anonymity for their subscribers, allowing time to explore the profiles of other users and hopefully in the end to find the perfect soul mate. However there are often unintended consequences leading to disappointment, and, in some cases, sad endings.

Karl Bruchmeier was having a cup of tea with his upstairs neighbour Marjorie Taylor, "I've met lots of lovely young women since I moved here. It's really changed my life."

"That's good news, Karl, I'm so pleased for you. But I never see you go out, so where did you meet these young ladies, and by young do you mean younger than you?"

"Sorry, Marjorie, what I should have said is I've been chatting to them online, and I haven't actually met any of them in person, yet. Most are in their twenties or early thirties, I believe."

Marjorie frowned, obviously puzzled, "On line? I'm not sure I've ever heard of that expression before. Do you mean on the telephone?"

Karl gave a knowing smile. "What it means, Marjorie, is that when I connect to the Internet on my computer I chat to them on a dating site."

"Ah, I see, or rather I don't see. All this computer stuff is beyond me."

A retired accounts clerk, now in his late fifties, Karl had been 'made redundant' some twenty-five years earlier and had never worked since. Whenever Marjorie asked him about the circumstances of his redundancy and his failure to find another job, he always changed the subject. A tall, slim built man, with his wispy grey hair worn long over the collar with a few stray strands over his ears, he always wore a Southampton FC baseball cap to cover his bald patch. Perhaps, Marjorie thought, he even wore the cap in bed?

Marjorie's daughter, Alicia, was sure Karl wore most of his late father's clothes, - very 1940s, very

Germanic. She often described Karl as 'sadly lacking in both humour and social skills, probably largely due to a childhood diet comprising too much sauerkraut.'

From the age of four onwards the daily diet of sauerkraut and boiled pork for lunch and dinner inevitably resulted in excessive flatulence as well as bad breath, which meant that Karl was quite a lonely child at the Daffodils Pre-school Nursery. The die was cast in those early years, and as time passed he became increasingly withdrawn, a loner. Throughout his school years, from Westfield Lane First School onwards, the inability to develop normal relationships with others was not helped, for example, when by the time he was twelve, other boys wore smart grey long trousers at school and jeans at other times, while he was still in lederhosen. Post-puberty, that is from the age of fifteen, although the lederhosen had been ditched, he really didn't have a lot going for him when it came to dating the opposite sex.

He was the only child of parents Ulrich and Heike Bruchmeier who came to the UK from Germany in 1950. Other than three years at university, Karl had always lived with his Mutti und Vati.

Shortly after they died, both in their late eighties, he sold the family home in Southampton, and moved into a one-bedroomed ground-floor flat in Bognor Regis. Now alone, he led a very reclusive life, rarely venturing out of his front door other than on Monday mornings to put his bin out for collection. Groceries were delivered by Ocado.

Apart from his laptop computer, which was at least the means of some anonymous interaction with the world outside of 24 Lyndholme Street, the only real-person social contact Karl had was an occasional cup of tea with Marjorie, who had been widowed for the past thirty years. In Karl's mind she had become almost like a replacement mother.

He often spoke about his parents, and how their experiences during the Second World War had shaped the rest of their lives. Of course, having been born in UK, Karl had no knowledge of how they came to be living here, nor why they had chosen to settle in West Sussex.

Apparently throughout the war Ulrich had served with the Wehrmacht 7th Panzer Division where he had been a mechanic servicing Tiger tanks, dangerous but not very exciting work. Dangerous because he was by profession a dentist, so that he was used to taking things out but never putting them back, which, to state the obvious, was highly dangerous for the crews of tanks serviced by Panzergrenadier First Class Bruchmeier! On the other hand, Heike had been a telephone operator in the Berlin Führer Bunker which was both dangerous and exciting. Dangerous largely because of its infamous residents. Nearing the end of the war, Heike had escaped Berlin just in time to avoid capture by the Russians, and had eventually made it back to her home town of Rothenburg which was where she met and married Ulrich.

On the occasions when he visited Marjorie, Karl talked about his wish to find a wife and perhaps raise a family, which of course would be a mirror image of his own upbringing. It wasn't at all clear whether any such marriage might result in any children being subjected to wearing hand-me-down lederhosen.

When speaking about his exchanges on various Internet dating websites, he would become very animated, quite contrary to his normal very dour demeanour. "I've made any number of promising contacts online Marjorie, lots of lovely blonde girls, very revealing pictures. One of them in particular says she likes me a lot."

Marjorie smiled and nodded; she'd heard all this before. "And where do these girls come from? Are they local?"

"Oh no, not local, I've never seen girls as beautiful as these in West Sussex. They're either from the Ukraine or Russia."

"I see," said Marjorie, "and what's the cost of all this to you Karl?"

"Oh, not much," he replied, "and in any case, I'm sure it'll be worth it in the end... ten pounds each time I log on, I think."

Marjorie was shocked. What a terrible waste of money. However it didn't come as a complete surprise as Alicia had told her as much before. "That seems very expensive to me my dear. I always thought all this Internet business was free? Of course, I suppose it also depends how often you use it?"

Karl was no longer quite so animated, "Do you know, Marjorie, I never thought of it that way before. Skype would probably be the nearest low-cost messaging, but then I don't know how it works."

Marjorie was relishing this. Of course, she meant to be helpful to Karl, who she guessed was probably in quite a lot of debt, and she did, after all, feel a degree of responsibility. He was so helpless.

"Well? How often Karl?"

By now Karl was visibly squirming. The questions were making him feel very uncomfortable, and embarrassed. "To tell you the truth, I've never given it a thought in terms of how much it was costing, I think possibly as many as four times a day."

"That's forty pounds in one day, and how many days in a week do you go onto these websites?" Marjorie might be getting on in years, but when it came to money matters she was sharper than most, and determined to make the point for his own good.

"Nearly..., every day..., Marjorie..., my God!" His complexion had turned as white as one of her fine cotton sheets - it didn't bear thinking about what the colour of his bed sheets might be.

"So. That's two hundred and eighty pounds a week, over a thousand pounds a month; no wonder you're hard up, Karl. Your father would turn over in his grave."

"Thanks for putting it that way, and you're absolutely right Marjorie. I must do something about it straight away."

With that, Karl got up and headed for the door. "Have to go now. I really can't thank you enough for your advice, as always."

"Good night Karl," she called after him. A half smile, and at the same time a worried frown crossed her face, showing how much she doubted he really would take her advice for once.

Two months later Marjorie heard a lot of noise outside so she looked out of the window that overlooked the street below. There was a large vehicle, like a car transporter, and two men were loading Karl's car onto the back. He appeared to be supervising the operation. This was the first time she had seen him since their conversation about the cost of the dating sites. Probably the car had broken down she thought. They must be taking it to the garage for repair.

That evening Marjorie's daughter Alicia called. "Hi, Mum. How are you today?"

"I'm fine thanks. Darling, you know Karl in the ground-floor flat?"

"Yes, Mum. Is he okay?"

"Well, I think he is, haven't seen him for ages. I wondered whether I'd upset him by mentioning the cost of all these websites he seems to spend so much time on."

"Probably, Mum, but then that's his choice. Did you tell him I think those girls he chats to online aren't real? It's a joke, and he must have a really vivid imagination if you ask me. I read somewhere that it's probably some dirty old man with a load of photographs and a computer living in a bedsit somewhere in South London..., and laughing all the way to the bank no doubt."

"No, darling, I didn't say anything, only that I thought it was expensive. I hadn't seen him for weeks until I saw him outside this morning when his car was taken away for repair."

Alicia laughed, "From what you've told me before, Mum, I somehow think the car doesn't need repair, he never uses it. Wouldn't surprise me if he's been made bankrupt and the creditors will have taken it. In that case, I wonder if he even managed to hang onto his laptop?"

* * *

Alicia was quite right. In the following week's local newspaper under legal notices, there was the confirmation that Karl had been declared bankrupt, and the creditors obviously wanted to establish their first claim on any assets.

The weeks passed and Marjorie hadn't seen hide nor hair of Karl since the day his car was taken away on the low loader. She'd tried a few times to call him on the telephone and left messages asking whether he was okay, but he hadn't replied. She became very concerned; he had no family and to the best of her knowledge, no friends she might call on. Eventually she decided to call the police. Sergeant Morris was on duty; he was a nice man who she'd met on a number of occasions in the past at the Methodist Chapel.

"I haven't seen him in over six weeks now. He never goes out anywhere, but at the very least he would call me every few days. I wonder would it be possible for you to check and see if he's all right."

Sergeant Morris took note of Karl's description, the address and his landline number. "I'm sure there's a simple explanation, Mrs Taylor. But of course, we'll get a local patrol vehicle to call sometime during the day tomorrow. Don't you worry now, I'll call you the moment I hear something."

The following morning just before she put on the TV for the mid-day news, Marjorie looked out of the window and saw that a police car was parked in the street below. She then settled down with a cup of tea and watched the news followed by Doctors. Later that afternoon at about four o'clock, Marjorie looked out of the window again and much to her surprise, the police car was still outside. What on earth are they doing all this time?' she asked herself.

After tea, about six o'clock, the bell rang, and when she opened the door, there was Sergeant Morris and a young policewoman. "Hello Mrs Taylor. May we come in? This is WPC Anne Jordan."

"Yes of course. Would you like a cup of tea?"

"That would be nice, thank you, milk no sugar."

Marjorie turned the television off and five minutes later returned from the kitchen with tea and biscuits on a tray. Sergeant Morris and WPC Jordan were sat on the sofa.

"Thanks for the tea, Mrs Taylor. I'm sorry to disturb you at this hour, but I'm afraid we've bad news about Mr Bruchmeier. I'm sorry to say that he died. That's the reason why you haven't heard from him."

Marjorie burst into a of flood tears "Oh God, no." She sobbed. "I had a feeling something was wrong. How did he die? If only I'd said something sooner… "

"Come now Mrs Taylor, you did absolutely the

right thing. As for what's happened I'm afraid we're unable to say anything further at this stage. Anne will stay with you for a while, and she's always available to help should you feel the need."

It took another two months before poor Karl could be buried. First of all the police seemed to spend days downstairs; then there was a Post Mortem, followed by an Inquest which resulted in a verdict of suicide caused by an overdose of methadone. There were some quite bizarre facts unveiled in the police evidence given by Sergeant Morris. Apparently Karl was found on the floor of his sitting room wearing rather ill-fitting lederhosen and a baseball cap. The room had been in a complete mess. It was as though a tornado had passed through. On the floor next to him there was an empty bottle of methadone, which had been prescribed some time ago for his late mother; his hand still gripped a heavy hammer which he appeared to have used to destroy his laptop computer. The hammer had also been used to smash a framed photograph of Heike during her time in the Berlin Führer Bunker flanked on the one side by a sombre looking Adolf Hitler and on the other by an equally serious-looking Eva Braun-Hitler. Shortly after the photograph was taken, they were of course, to become the late Mr and Mrs Hitler. The only book in the flat was a well-thumbed copy of Mein Kampf.

* * *

On the day of Karl's funeral, the only ones at the cemetery were Marjorie, Alicia, Sergeant Morris and WPC Jordan. As they returned to the car, Alicia walked along slowly, chatting to Anne, who she hadn't met before, "In the end he had no one you know. I never ever thought anything like this would happen. Suicide. It's so so sad."

Alicia offered to stay with Marjorie for a few days until things settled down a bit. She was a great comfort to her mum in the circumstances. On Monday morning of the following week, Alicia went to Sainsbury's, shopping to make sure Mum didn't run short of food after she left to go home. As she was unloading the car, a taxi drew up alongside and the driver called over, "Excuse me miss. Is this number twenty-four?"

"Yes it is. Can I help you?" Alicia replied.

The driver got out of the cab and opened the rear door. His passenger got out. She was tall, about five eight, with long blonde hair, Alicia guessed in her early thirties, an absolute stunner just as Karl would have said. She smiled and extended her hand.

"Hello..., my name is Valentina Akulov, a friend of Mr Karl Bruchmeier. Mmmm, how to say..., I am..., mmm..., sorry..., but my English is not very good."

Epilogue

The journey through to completion of Migrating Geese has been at times quite tortuous, and has caused Jean, my long-suffering sounding board, a severe pain in the ear. Will I ever be forgiven?

I know that there is no such thing as the perfect story, and there has to be the time when one makes the decision to finally call a halt to the process of drafting, editing, re-drafting, and sometimes starting all over again. This time has been no different.

Naturally there isn't 'time to stop and stare' and as a result of encouragement from readers of The Gregory Journal who wanted to know the full life story of my great-uncle William, work on a novel 'Gregory re-visited' has already started. The actual title is yet to be agreed.

In the pipeline are two further pieces :

A further anthology of short stories will include :

- Edward (aged 16) and… Now I know. Edward finally understands the meaning of life (with help from Digger and the nice Mrs Prudholme}

- My Dad's Army

- Rudy and Sid

- The Mind Eurochip

- The Clairvoyant

- Frank's BOHICA moment

- The Baby Alarm

The Kensington Connection is a story of duplicity, fraud, the selling of defence secrets to enemies of the UK, and the murder of a leading Westminster Politician at his apartment in Kensington.

To assist the programme of continuing improvement, readers' comments will be greatly appreciated either online at www.jonmoorthorpe.com or to the Publisher's address at the front of this book.

About the Author

John Sykes (pen named Jon Moorthorpe) was born in the coal mining village of Moorthorpe, West Yorkshire, seventy-four years ago.

He has lead a life full of very different experiences, which have stood him in good stead when recently he decided to turn to writing and many of his stories are largely based on real events, only names and locations have been changed, to protect the guilty!

He started his working life as a junior reporter on a local weekly newspaper (see stories about Edward), then spent fifteen years in the Regular

Army, followed for the next thirty years working in the Defence Industry He was Chairman of the Equality for Veterans Association for five years until stepping down due to ill health.

John has four children and six grandchildren and lives with his partner Jean in West Sussex.

Reviews of Jon Moorthorpe's 'The Gregory Journal'

William Gregory was born in Lancashire in 1879 and later emigrated to Canada. He returned to England in 1916 serving as a Private with the Nova Scotia Regiment, Canadian Infantry. He took part in the Battles for Messines Ridge and Hill 70. Dates and places are factual, the diary entries are the product of the Author's imagination. William was Jon Moorthorpe's Great Uncle.

> *"It showed a realistic view of what it would be like to live in the trenches in the Great War. My heart broke a little when I got to the end."*
>
> **Tom Millman**

"A clever account of the build-up and anticipation of what fighting at the front in the trenches mean to ordinary men like William Gregory. The diary entries are evocative and tinglingly real. A little gem worth reading even just for the twist at the end. Brilliantly crafted."

Jeremy Good

"What men at the front had to put up with apart from the Germans is brought home in this diary. A moving and nostalgic account."

Alicia Scanlon

"Much better than many other widely published WW1 books I've read."

Sandra Lyons

"A really good short story bringing personal thoughts of a WW1 soldier to life. Born in Lancashire but serving with a Canadian Regiment adds an interesting twist to the story."

Margaret Walker